THE CASE OF THE MONKEYS THAT FELL FROM THE TREES

THE CASE OF THE MONKEYS THAT FELL FROM THE TREES

and Other Mysteries in Tropical Nature

BY SUSAN E. QUINLAN

Boyds Mills Press

To my extraordinary mother, Lola F. Quinlan, my beloved
daughters, Willow and Summer, and to all the scientists
upon whose hard work this book is based.

—S. E. Q.

Text and illustrations copyright © 2003 by Susan E. Quinlan
All rights reserved

Published by Boyds Mills Press, Inc.
A Highlights Company
815 Church Street
Honesdale, Pennsylvania 18431
Printed in China
Visit our Web site at www.boydsmillspress.com

Publisher Cataloging-in-Publication Data (U.S)
Quinlan, Susan E.
The case of the monkeys that fell from the trees : and other mysteries in
tropical nature / by Susan E. Quinlan.—1st ed.
[172] p. : ill. ; cm.
Includes bibliographical references and index.
Summary: Description of scientific research that explains tropical phenomena.
ISBN 1-56397-902-0
1. Tropics—Juvenile literature. 2. Ecology—Tropics—Juvenile literature.
3. Nature—Tropics—Juvenile literature. (1. Tropics. 2. Ecology—Tropics.
3. Nature—Tropics.) I. Title.
508.313 21   2003
2002108914

First edition, 2003
The text of this book is set in 14-point Caslon 224 Book.

10 9 8 7 6 5 4 3 2

In appreciation

This book would not have been possible without the many tropical forest researchers who originally recognized these mysteries, asked the right questions, and did all the difficult investigative work in search of understanding. I would like to express particular appreciation to the following scientists who kindly helped me write these stories about their discoveries:

Kenneth E. Glander, Ph.D., Director, Duke University Primate Center; Daniel Janzen, Ph.D., Department of Biology, University of Pennsylvania; Lawrence E. Gilbert, Ph.D., Section of Integrative Biology, The University of Texas; John W. Daly, Ph.D., National Academy of Sciences USA; Neal Griffith Smith, Ph.D., Staff Scientist Emeritus, Smithsonian Tropical Research Institute; Thomas S. Ray, Ph.D., Department of Zoology, University of Oklahoma; Henry F. Howe, Ph.D., Department of Biological Sciences, University of Illinois at Chicago; Alejandro Estrada, Ph.D., Estacion de Biologia Los Tuxtlas, Instituto de Biologia, Mexico; Ariadna Valentina Lopes, Ph.D., Departamento de Botanica, Universidade Federal de Pernambuco, Brasil; and Isabel Cristina Machado, Ph.D., Departmento de Botanica, Universidade Federal de Pernambuco, Brasil.

Additional review of the text for factual content and accuracy was done by Susan Moegenburg, Ph.D., Research Associate, Smithsonian Migratory Bird Center. I thank Kent Brown Jr. for supporting this project, editor Greg Linder for his reviews and criticisms of the manuscript, and Alice Cummiskey for working the extra mile to see production through to the presses. Special thanks to Sven-Olof Lindblad for giving me several opportunities to discover tropical forests firsthand.

Finally, my sincere thanks to all my family and friends who helped me keep the ups and downs of this project in perspective. I am particularly grateful to my husband, Bud Lehnhausen, who continually encouraged and supported my work. He also generously shared his many photographs of tropical wildlife as artwork references. I also thank my daughters for allowing me the many, many hours of work time I needed to complete this undertaking.

Susan E. Quinlan

CONTENTS

INTRODUCTION

IMAGINE VISITING a tropical forest. Picture towering trees reaching their emerald green foliage upward to catch the sun's bright rays. Walk under the trees into the dimly lit forest depths. Breathe the hot, muggy air and smell the heavy scent of rich greenery and perfumed flowers.

Giant gray tree trunks, massive roots, twisted rope-like vines, and scraggly young trees crowd the dark interior of the forest. A thin carpet of wet, dead leaves lies underfoot. Look up to see giant tree branches draped with strange gardens of vines, ferns, orchids,

9

cacti, and pineapple-like plants. Listen! Do you hear the raucous cries of parrots rushing overhead? The soft, tinkling call of a tree frog? The steady, rattling buzz of a cicada? You may not see these or any other animals just now. But there are hundreds, probably thousands, of creatures around you in this forest. You are in the midst of the richest of all Earth's ecosystems.

Biologists who study these amazing forests are drawn back to them again and again. The very real possibility of finding some previously undiscovered species is one lure. But most biologists are intrigued by a much larger mystery: How and why do so many kinds of plants and animals live in tropical forests? And how do these remarkable ecosystems work?

Through the work of hundreds of scientists, each studying how various species survive and interact with other creatures and their environment, a new understanding of tropical forests is slowly emerging. This book is intended to help you share in that understanding. Each chapter presents a tropical forest mystery. You can consider the findings of investigating scientists and discover how their research has revealed one or more of the hidden connections that make tropical forests so fascinating—and so fragile.

Why do monkeys sometimes fall from the trees? How do passionflower vines foil their predators? How

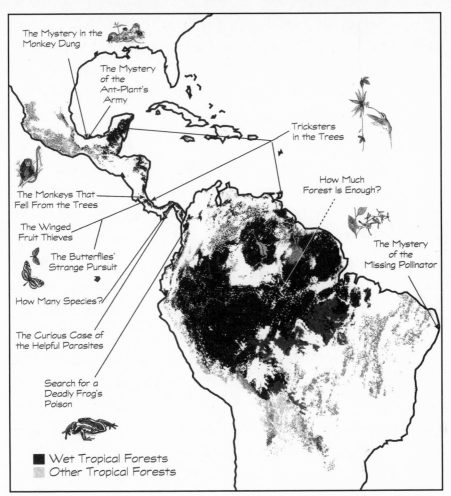

The Mystery in the Monkey Dung

The Mystery of the Ant-Plant's Army

Tricksters in the Trees

How Much Forest Is Enough?

The Monkeys That Fell From the Trees

The Winged Fruit Thieves

The Butterflies' Strange Pursuit

The Mystery of the Missing Pollinator

How Many Species?

The Curious Case of the Helpful Parasites

Search for a Deadly Frog's Poison

■ Wet Tropical Forests
░ Other Tropical Forests

This map shows the locations of the main research studies described in this book. Though all of the projects discussed herein were conducted in tropical forests of Central and South America (New World tropical forests), the connections revealed are representative of those found in tropical forest ecosystems around the world.

11

do poison dart frogs make their poisons? These are just a few of the questions scientists have asked while attempting to understand how tropical forests work. All the mysteries discussed in this book are from the tropical forests of Central and South America, but similar mysteries and interconnections exist in tropical forests throughout the world.

By the time you reach the end of this book, you will see why biologists now regard tropical forests as far more than amazing collections of plants and animals. If you think about all the hidden connections their work has revealed, you may also begin to understand how Earth's orchestra of living creatures continuously re-creates and maintains the symphony of life that exists in tropical forests—and in nature all around us.

WHERE ARE
ALL THE ANIMALS?

WHEN YOU THINK about tropical forests, you probably imagine colorful macaws and toucans, leaping monkeys and creeping jaguars, venomous snakes, carnivorous fish, and giant insects. All of these creatures do live in tropical forests, along with a tremendous variety of less familiar animals, plants, and fungi. In fact, scientists estimate that well over half of all species on Earth reside in tropical forests even though these forests cover less than 7 percent of the Earth's land. Yet if you visited a tropical forest, you might be surprised to see few animals at first.

Henry Walter Bates was one of the first European naturalists to explore the tropical forests along the Amazon River in Brazil. He reported his puzzling first

15

impressions in 1848: "We were disappointed . . . in not meeting with any of the larger animals in the forest. There was no tumultuous movement or sound of life. We did not see or hear monkeys, and no tapir or jaguar crossed our path. Birds, also, appeared to be exceedingly scarce." Like Bates, many tropical forest visitors today ask, "Where are all the animals?" You need to know more about tropical forests to discover the answer to this question and to truly appreciate the wealth of life they harbor.

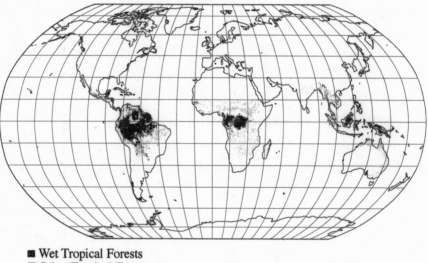

■ Wet Tropical Forests
■ Other Tropical Forests

The extent of tropical forests remaining worldwide in 2001 based on information excerpted with permission from the "Global Distribution of Current Forests" map produced by the United Nations Environment Program-World Conservation Monitoring Centre, Cambridge, U.K.

Tropical forests exist at or close to the equator, and can be found in Africa, Asia, Indonesia, northern Australia, Central and South America, and on many tropical islands around the world. All of these regions receive close to twelve hours of intense sunlight every day throughout the year. However, other environmental conditions vary from place to place, so there are many kinds of tropical forest.

Tropical Wet Forest (Rain Forest)   *Tropical Cloud Forest*   *Tropical Dry Forest*

Many kinds of tropical forests exist around the world. This book focuses primarily on those found in Central and South America (the New World).

Hot, wet rain forests occur at low elevations, including on lands along the Amazon River, in coastal areas of

Australia, and on many Indonesian islands. These forests get drenched by more than one hundred inches of rainfall each year and temperatures hover close to 80° Fahrenheit day and night.

Tropical forests on high mountain slopes are cool and foggy. They are sometimes called cloud forests. Air temperatures here may rise above 60°F in the daytime but plummet to 45°F or colder at night. Clouds scatter the sun's intense rays and bathe the treetops in dew, so the canopy continually drips water onto the forest floor. The branches of most trees in these forests are heavily laden with lichens, orchids, ferns, and other plants. Many kinds of fungi also flourish.

Dry tropical forests occur wherever heavy rainfall is limited to certain times of year. Although the trees in these forests are green and wet during the rainy season, many shed their leaves during the dry season. All the creatures that live in these forests must be able to survive periods of drought.

Some tropical forests are flooded with several feet of water for half the year or more, while others are never flooded. Some grow on rich volcanic soils, while others thrive on nutrient-poor sands. In many respects, every patch of tropical forest is unique, because the geologic history, soil type, water drainage, local climate, and plant and animal life may vary widely from site to site, even within a small geographic area.

All tropical forests have distinct seasons, but the fairly constant and intense year-round supply of sunlight fuels lush plant growth. Plants, including trees, trap the sun's energy, storing some of it in their leaves, flowers, fruits, branches, stems, trunks, and roots. These all become food for the other living things in a forest. An acre of tropical forest produces more vegetation each year than an acre of any other natural habitat. You might expect such an abundant food supply to support many more animals per acre than other habitats, but this does not appear to be the case.

Scientists have tried to estimate the animal biomass—the total weight of all animals—in an acre of tropical forest. To do this, they counted all the birds, mammals, amphibians, insects, and other animals they could find in a small area, then multiplied the number of each by the average weight of an animal of that species.

Different scientists working in different tropical forests arrived at similarly low estimates of animal biomass. Their results suggest that an acre of tropical forest may contain only a little more animal biomass than an acre of temperate forest—and far less than an acre of some African grasslands. Why this might be so remains a mystery.

Some scientists suspect that tropical forest researchers missed counting many of the animals present, because this is such a difficult task. If so, the low estimates of animal biomass might be incorrect. However, other scientists think the estimates reflect the true situation.

How could tropical forests produce so much plantlife and hold such a great diversity of animal species, yet contain only a modest amount of animal biomass? Consider the findings of ornithologist James Karr. Using the methods described above, Karr calculated the biomass of birds in a tropical forest in Panama. He also calculated the biomass in a temperate forest in Illinois. The two figures were similar—about 116 pounds of birds per one hundred acres in the tropical forest versus 107 pounds per one hundred acres in the Illinois forest. However, Karr counted far more bird species and breeding pairs in the Panamanian forest.

How could more birds add up to about the same biomass? For one thing, Karr found that the tropical birds were much smaller on average than the birds in Illinois. Although large macaws and toucans were present in low numbers, most of the tropical birds he observed were small species like hummingbirds, flycatchers, manakins, and antbirds.

Secondly, about two-fifths of the bird species in the tropical forest occurred irregularly or in low numbers, compared to only one-fifth of the species in Illinois. The irregular tropical species wandered through large areas of forest in search of patchy sources of food, such as fruiting trees, nectar-filled flowers, or swarms of insects. Since these species occurred only in low numbers, Karr rarely saw them.

Many other kinds of animals also occur only in low numbers in tropical forests. This is surprising, since tropical forests are green year-round and appear to offer a continuous, abundant supply of food for plant-eating animals. But recent research suggests that this appearance is an illusion. Scientists have discovered that monthly variations in rainfall, cloud cover, and winds greatly affect the availability of fruit, new leaves, and other foods for wildlife.

Small birds, like hummingbirds, flycatchers, funarids, manakins, and antbirds, are far more common in tropical forests than such large bird species as macaws or toucans. Many species, large and small, are uncommon and wander through large forest areas.

While working in the forest of Cocha Cashu, Peru, scientist John Terborgh discovered that many animals face an annual shortage of food. Only twelve of some one thousand species of trees there contain any fruit during a few months at the end of the annual rainy season. During this period of fruit scarcity, over half of all the large animal species in the forest have to rely on just a few species of fruiting trees. This period of food scarcity greatly reduces the number of animals the Cocha Cashu forest can support. Among the animals affected are peccaries, bats, opossums, agoutis, macaws, toucans, and several species of monkeys. Similar periods of resource scarcity may limit most populations of tropical forest wildlife.

Fruit is scarce at certain times of every year, making it difficult for capuchin monkeys and other fruit-eating mammals to find enough food.

Additional factors may also be involved. Some scientists suspect that the large number and variety of predators in these forests may keep prey

22

populations low. Others think that much of the vegetation in tropical forests is either inedible or difficult for most animals to digest. Whatever the reasons, many tropical birds, mammals, reptiles, amphibians, and insects need very large areas of forest to survive and are present only in low numbers.

The low numbers of many of the species present is certainly one reason that tropical forest visitors often see few animals. Wildlife viewing is also difficult because animals in tropical forests have lots of places to hide. Giant roots and tree trunks, draping vines, and low light levels in the forest depths allow visitors to see only a short distance. Even nearby animals can be completely hidden.

In addition, only a few large animals live on the floor of tropical forests. In Central and South American forests, for example, deer, agoutis, and tapirs are among the few ground-dwelling species. This is because most of the

A tapir is one of few large animals species that live on the ground in tropical forests.

edible flowers, fruits, and young leaves grow only in the upper reaches of the forest, called the canopy. As a result, more than half the animal species in tropical forests live in the treetops. You must strain your neck and peer straight up with binoculars if you want to glimpse parrots, toucans, monkeys, anteaters, opossums, sloths, or jaguars. Even frogs, snakes, lizards, and insects live up high.

Like this tamandua, or arboreal anteater, more than half the animal species in tropical forests live high up in the forest canopy.

Like this moth, many tropical forest animals are difficult to spot as they blend in with their surroundings through camouflaging coloration and behaviors.

To further complicate wildlife viewing, many tropical forest animals are well camouflaged. The white spots on a paca's brown back and the dark velvet coat of a tapir help both animals disappear into the forest shadows. The greenish algae that grows in a sloth's grooved hairs helps this slow-moving mammal blend in with the foliage. Snakes that hang from tree branches look like drooping vines. Small bats that shingle tree trunks look like brown, furry bark. Even brilliant green parrots and bright blue and yellow honeycreepers disappear when they land in trees full of glistening green leaves and shifting shadows. Tropical forest insects also have countless ways of disappearing. Moths look like dead leaves, katydids like live ones. Certain bugs resemble twigs, while beetles may look like tree bark or flower buds. If you don't look carefully and patiently, you won't see any of these forest creatures.

A final reason visitors often see few animals is that many tropical forest creatures are nocturnal, becoming active only at night. About half of all mammal species in the tropical forests of Central and South America are bats. Only dusk brings these creatures out of their hiding places in hollow trees, under leaves, and within forest crannies. Nighthawks and potoos, night herons, and owls join the bats for nighttime hunting. Many snakes and frogs also move around mainly at night. Even flying insects swarm in the dark. Moths, mosquitoes, flies, beetles, wasps, and bees fill the tropical night air with wings. Most visitors rethink their first impression when they hear the wild uproar of hums, buzzes, croaks, tinkles, and screams that every night in the forest brings.

After Henry Walter Bates had spent a few months along the Amazon, his disappointment turned into amazement. Bates knew that only sixty-six kinds of butterflies lived in all of the British Isles, a land area of over 120,000 square miles. He was astonished to find more than seven hundred kinds of butterflies within just one hour's walk from his house near the mouth of the Amazon. Fascinated, Bates remained in the region for several years. During that time, he discovered and

Many tropical forest animals are active only at night.

described over eight thousand animal species (mostly insects) that were previously unknown to science.

During the 150 or so years since Bates studied the Amazon forests, scientists have discovered many thousands more new plant and animal species in tropical forests there and around the world. Bird-watchers have recorded nearly six hundred bird species in just a fifty-five-square-mile area of forest in Peru. That number isn't much smaller than the total of seven hundred bird species found in all of North America. Barro Colorado, a four thousand-acre forested island in the Panama Canal, is home to more species of frogs than all of the states in the western United States combined. Insect scientist Edward O. Wilson identified more species of ants from a single tree in Peru than occur in the entire British Isles.

The total number of animal species that live in tropical forests remains unknown. The more carefully scientists comb through these forests, the more new species they discover. Even during the 1990s, scientists encountered several new species of birds, mammals, and frogs, as well as hundreds of new insect species. Some research suggests that the number of yet-to-be-discovered arthropod species (insects, spiders, centipedes, mites, and other joint-legged animals) is in the millions. Without question, tropical forests are home to far more plants, birds, mammals, reptiles, and insects than any other environment on Earth.

HOW
MANY
SPECIES?

SCIENTISTS DID NOT truly appreciate the incredible diversity of life in tropical forests until the early 1970s. That is when insect biologists Terry Erwin and Janice Scott attempted to find out how many and which kinds of insects lived in a single species of tropical tree. Using a powerful spray gun, they sent fogs of poison gas into the leaves and branches of nineteen *Luhea* trees growing in tropical forests in Panama.

Within a few minutes, a rain of thousands of dead and dying insects poured down from each tree. The researchers collected most of the falling insects in large funnels that dropped them into alcohol-filled bottles. The alcohol preserved the insects for later study. Erwin and Scott repeated this procedure in the nineteen trees at three different times of year.

Back in the laboratory, they carefully sorted through their samples, separating all the insects according to the exact tree they came from, the date they fell, and the insect group (beetles, leafhoppers, ants, and others) to which they belonged. The scientists called in many experts to help them sort and identify the samples, because the total number of insects and species was staggering.

For example, the beetles collected from beneath a single tree included more than 2,000 individuals belonging to 335 species. The researchers' total collection of beetles from all nineteen trees included more than 7,700 individuals of nearly

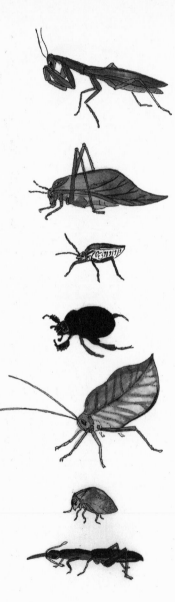

These insects are just a few of the staggering variety of invertebrate life forms found in tropical forests.

1,000 different species. Each tree and each time of year yielded a very different collection of insect species! Many of the species collected were new to science.

Based on his collection of beetles from *Luhea* trees and his knowledge of tropical insect biology, Erwin estimated that 163 beetle species might live in *Luhea* trees and nowhere else. Considering the estimated 50,000 tropical-tree species worldwide, and assuming that other tree species might have similar numbers of dependent beetle species, Erwin calculated that more than 8 million species of beetles might exist in tropical forest treetops.

Out of curiosity, Erwin used this information to estimate how many other arthropod species might exist in tropical forests. He reasoned that beetles make up about three-eighths of all known species of arthropods, and some portion of beetles and arthropods live in the soil, not in the treetops. Considering these factors and others, Erwin calculated a rough estimate of the number of arthropod species in tropical forests: an astounding 30 million. Other scientists had previously estimated that, at most, 1.5 million species of animals of all kinds exist on the entire Earth.

Today Erwin's estimate remains under some debate as scientists work to arrive at more precise calculations. The exact number of arthropod species will never be known. But in many ways it does not matter whether the number is 5 million, 10 million, 30 million, or 80 million. Erwin's work clearly revealed that the invertebrate life in tropical forests is far more diverse than anyone had previously imagined.

THE CASE OF
THE MONKEYS
THAT FELL
FROM THE TREES

WHEN THE INCIDENTS began in August 1972, biologist Ken Glander and his wife, Molly, had been studying the eating habits of a troop of howling monkeys in northwestern Costa Rica for nearly three months. Then, over a two-week period, seven monkeys from various troops in the area fell out of trees and died. Another fell but climbed back up.

One morning the Glanders watched a female howling monkey with a ten-day-old baby turn in tight circles on a tree branch. Abruptly, she fell off the branch. For a moment she hung upside down, suspended by her long tail. Then her grip failed and she plunged thirty-five feet to the forest floor. Dazed but still alive, she climbed back up, carrying her clinging infant. She stopped on a thick branch and sat there without eating for the next twenty-four hours.

Normally, howling monkeys are skilled, nimble climbers. They often leap ten feet or more between tree limbs, and they almost never fall. Why were monkeys suddenly falling from trees?

Glander wondered if a disease or parasite might be involved. He asked scientists in the microbiology department at the University of Costa Rica to examine some of the dead monkeys and look for clues. The scientists found no signs of disease or parasites. Nor had the monkeys starved. All had died in apparently healthy condition. Glander began to think they had been poisoned. But who or what would poison wild monkeys? Glander had several green, leafy suspects in mind, all of them tropical forest trees.

Many tropical trees have similar-looking leaves and trunks, so it is difficult to determine their species. But tropical plant expert Paul Opler had identified all the trees in the Glanders' study area. Several poisonous species were present. Suspiciously, some of the

The scientists followed a troop of howling monkeys around, carefully recording exactly which trees they visited, and exactly what they ate.

monkeys that fell had been feeding in trees known to have poisonous leaves. Yet Glander knew this proved nothing.

All plants produce chemicals called secondary compounds, many of which are poisonous. Plants make these chemicals for a variety of purposes. Some ward off plant-eating animals, especially insects. But howling monkeys eat nothing except plants, so they could not survive unless they were able to digest or tolerate plant poisons. Other scientists had observed howlers eating leaves from many kinds of trees, including poisonous species, without any signs of distress. As a result, most scientists assumed that howling monkeys had an unlimited food supply in their lush tropical forest homes. Glander wasn't so sure.

The monkeys that fell from the trees strengthened his belief that howling monkeys could not eat leaves from just any tree. He suspected that certain trees were monkey killers, but he needed evidence before he could point fingers. He and Molly began collecting the data they needed to make a case.

Their days started around 4 or 5 A.M. That's when the monkeys awoke, often greeting the day with roars and growls. The monkeys soon set off, alternating bouts of feeding with periods of crawling, leaping, and climbing through the treetops. Wherever the monkeys went, the Glanders followed on foot.

At midday, the monkeys settled down. Draping themselves over large branches, their arms and legs dangling, the howlers slept with their tails wrapped around branches to anchor them in place. Late in the day, when the air cooled a few degrees, the monkeys stirred. They climbed and fed until settling down for the night at sunset.

For twelve months, the Glanders endured long days, mosquitoes, heavy rains, and temperatures that sometimes soared over 100°F. They did this in order to make their observations of the monkey troop as continuous as possible. Throughout each day, they recorded how many minutes the monkeys spent sleeping, eating, and moving. They recorded which of 1,699 individually numbered trees the monkeys slept in and ate from, and exactly which parts the monkeys ate—leaves, fruits, flowers, or stems.

Each day, the scientists collected samples of leaves from every tree the monkeys fed in that day, and leaves from nearby trees of the same species. The monkeys had visited these trees but did not feed in them. The Glanders tagged the leaves with wire labels, noting the tree, the date, and the time that the sample was collected. Next, they dried the leaves in an oven, then packed them in zippered plastic bags for later study.

The Glanders soon noticed that the howlers ate new leaves whenever they could, only occasionally eating fruits, flowers, or mature leaves. In certain trees, the monkeys plucked off the leaves, then stripped and tossed away the leaf blades. They ate

In certain trees, like cashew, howling monkeys eat only the leaf stems, tossing the leaf blades away. Are they wasting food?

only the remaining leaf stems. Other scientists thought this messy feeding behavior meant that howling monkeys could afford to be wasteful in a forest where food was so abundant. Glander wasn't convinced.

After thousands of hours of field work, including nearly two thousand hours of observing monkeys, Glander reviewed all the records he and Molly had gathered. Their careful data showed that howlers had not eaten leaves from just any trees in the forest. Indeed, the monkeys had rarely eaten leaves from the most common tree species. Instead, they spent most of their feeding time in a few uncommon kinds of trees. All told, the monkeys had eaten from only 331 of the 1,699 trees in the area. More surprisingly, they had spent three-quarters of their feeding time in just 88 trees. The data showed that the monkeys selected only certain tree species for feeding.

Glander discovered something even more surprising. The monkeys had not eaten leaves from all the trees of favored species. Instead, they ate leaves from just a few individual trees of most species. For example, the monkeys traveled through most of the 149 madera negra trees in the area, but they ate mature leaves from only three of these. This pattern fascinated Glander, because the madera negra is one of the most toxic trees in the forest. Its leaves are used to make rat poison.

To learn more, Glander chemically analyzed all the leaves he and Molly had collected from the madera negra trees in the study area during their field studies. The results were startling. The three individual trees from which the monkeys had eaten mature leaves showed no traces of poison alkaloids. But leaves collected from the other madera negras were packed with these poisons. Somehow, the monkeys had picked out those very few trees whose leaves were not poisonous.

Chemical analyses of mature leaves from other kinds of trees revealed a similar pattern. The howling monkeys had consistently selected the most nutritious, most digestible, and least poisonous leaves available in their patch of forest. Glander noted that howlers ate only the leaf stems in some trees because the stems contained fewer poisons than the leaves. His data showed that instead of being sloppy eaters awash in a sea of food, howling monkeys are cautious, picky eaters in a forest filled with poisons.

But the mystery of the monkeys that fell from the trees was not solved. If howling monkeys can identify and avoid the most toxic leaves, why would they ever become poisoned and fall? Glander uncovered more clues by studying plants and their poisons.

The concentration of poison is not uniform among those plants that produce poisonous secondary compounds. The kinds and amounts of poison present vary widely among plant species, among individual plants of a single species, and even within the parts of a single plant. In fact, individual plants make varying amounts of poisons at different times of year and under different growing conditions. Some plants produce more poisons after their leaves or twigs are eaten by plant-eating animals. These same plants make fewer poisons if they are not damaged by plant-eaters. Due to these constant changes, Glander realized that monkeys could not simply learn which trees had poisonous leaves and which had edible ones. Their task was far more complicated. How did the monkeys do it?

Again, Glander found an answer in his field records. Howlers had fed in 331 of the trees in the study area, but they made only one stop in 104 of these trees. In each case, a solitary adult monkey visited the tree briefly, ate just a little bit, and then moved on. Glander thinks these monkeys were "sampling" the leaves for poisons. If the plant parts were toxic, they probably tasted bad or made the monkey who sampled them feel slightly ill. He suspects that each monkey troop finds out which trees currently have the least poisonous leaves by regularly and carefully sampling from trees throughout the area. By using this technique, the monkeys would avoid eating too many of the most toxic plant poisons.

Considering the ever-changing toxicity of the leaves in a forest, however, Glander reasoned that individual monkeys may sometimes make mistakes. They may eat too many of the wrong leaves. More importantly, when edible leaves are scarce due to unusual conditions, monkeys may be forced to eat leaves they wouldn't otherwise choose. Glander first saw monkeys falling from trees during a severe drought year, when the howlers' food choices were quite limited. Because some poisons produced by tropical plants affect animal muscles and nerves, eating the wrong leaves could certainly cause illness, dizziness, and deadly falls.

Today, after more than thirty years of studying monkeys, Ken Glander is convinced that the falling monkeys he and Molly observed were poisoned by eating leaves from the wrong trees at the wrong time. His work shows that a tropical forest is like a pantry filled with a mixture of foods and poisons. Only the most selective eaters can avoid the poisons and find enough edible food to survive.

However, the monkeys' poison-filled pantry has a silver lining. Poison chemicals used in small amounts often have medicinal value. Many human medicines contain plant poisons, including aspirin, quinine, atropine, morphine, digitoxin (a heart medicine), and cancer-fighting vincristine and paclitaxel. In fact, an estimated one-fourth of all medicines prescribed in the United States today come from plants.

Glander and other researchers have gathered some evidence that howlers and other monkeys sometimes select poisonous leaves for medicinal purposes, such as ridding themselves of parasites. Glander thinks scientists searching for new medicines for people might get some useful tips from howlers. The monkeys' behavior might help scientists select those plants most worth sampling.

THE
MYSTERY
OF AN
ANT-PLANT'S ARMY

FAT, SHARP THORNS bristle from the branches of the bullhorn acacia, a small tree that grows from southern Mexico to Costa Rica. Scientists call this tree an "ant-plant" because hordes of tiny ants live inside its thorns. In 1874, naturalist Thomas Belt determined that several species of ants, known as *Pseudomyrmex* ants, live only in the swollen thorns of bullhorn acacias. He discovered that these ants feed mainly on special nectar and protein bodies produced by the

49

acacia's leaves. Belt observed the ants swarm out and fiercely deliver painful bites to any creature that touched the plant. From this behavior, he concluded that the ants helped acacias survive by defending them from large and small leaf-eaters. According to Belt, these ants formed "a most efficient standing army" for the plant.

Other scientists dismissed Belt's conclusion. Why would an army of ants guard a plant? Naturalist W. M. Wheeler argued that acacia thorns just happened to be a good place for ants to live. He believed the ants attacked only because they were defending their own colonies. To him, the acacias' impressive thorns seemed defense enough to protect the trees from large browsing animals. He did not believe the ants protected acacias from small leaf-eaters, either. As evidence, he pointed to fifty-four kinds of insects and other invertebrates that live on bullhorn acacias. The ants are simply parasites that live by taking energy and nutrients from the tree, he argued. In his words, "The acacia has no more need of ants than a dog has need of fleas."

Scientists debated the question for almost ninety years, but no one was interested in going to Central America to do an experiment that could settle the argument. Then, in 1963, researcher Daniel Janzen noticed ants attacking insects that landed on the leaves of a bullhorn acacia near Veracruz, Mexico. He decided to investigate, choosing to study a single species of bullhorn acacia that is inhabited mainly by one species of *Pseudomyrmex* ant.

Janzen observed many acacias to see if large animals ate their leaves and twigs. He saw cows and burros browsing on their leaves and twigs during the dry season when ant numbers were low, and in cold weather when the ants were inactive. This proved that acacia thorns alone were not enough to ward off these large plant-eaters.

Janzen further noted that cows rarely nibbled branches from ant-occupied acacias when the ants were active. When he led a tame deer up to bullhorn acacias, it browsed the leaves but soon became irritated by the acacia ants attacking its muzzle and moved off to feed elsewhere. To Janzen, these observations suggested that ants do help bullhorn acacias by fending off large plant-eaters.

Janzen tallied the many kinds of beetles, grasshoppers, moths, and other small animals that live in or feed on bullhorn acacia. As Wheeler had noted, there were more than fifty species. That is quite a few, but Janzen knew of other tropical plants used by hundreds of insect species. Janzen had an idea for a simple

Irritating ant bites quickly discouraged a tame brocket deer from browsing on bullhorn acacias.

experiment after he accidentally destroyed the ant colonies of two acacia trees. A variety of insects quickly devoured the new shoots of these trees. Yet the shoots of nearby trees with intact ant colonies remained undamaged. He wondered, would more kinds of invertebrates eat acacias if the ants were absent? Janzen decided to remove all the ants from some acacias and record exactly what happened. He figured that if ants truly defend bullhorn acacias from insects, the trees without ants would do poorly. If not, the acacias without ants would fare just as well as those with ants.

The scientist set up twenty-two study plots in southern Mexico. He divided each plot into two or more subplots. In some of the plots, he simply mapped all the established trees. In others, he cut all the existing acacias so he could observe the growth of young shoots. In one subplot within each larger plot, he allowed ants to remain. In the adjacent subplots, he attempted to remove all the ant colonies. Janzen used an insecticide and fire to get rid of the ants in many plots. He discovered he also could remove ant colonies from acacias by clipping off all the large dead thorns with a pair of hedge clippers. Clipping took a lot of time, but since the thorn tips are dead, it did not harm the plants. Without the thorns to live in, the ant colonies died.

Janzen measured the growth of all the bullhorn acacias in his plots every one to two months over the next year. He recorded some amazing differences between the growth of antless acacias and the growth of ant-occupied acacias. During the dry season, rodents chewed off more than half the new shoots in one antless subplot, but did no damage to young shoots in a nearby ant-occupied subplot. Within five days after Janzen removed the ants from another

53

subplot, beetles, grasshoppers, and caterpillars ate all the acacia leaves off previously undamaged plants. These observations indicated that the ants did indeed protect bullhorn acacias from small leaf-eating animals.

Various rodents and insects quickly attacked the twigs and leaves of antless acacias.

Janzen discovered that the ants also helped these acacias compete with other plants. He noticed that many antless acacias became overgrown by vines— plants that grow to reach sunlight by using other plants for support. Their slender young trunks were bent under the weight and their leaves were too shaded to grow. In contrast, Janzen never found a

Antless acacias got shaded out by vines and other plants.

single ant-occupied acacia overgrown by vines. Instead, these acacias were typically surrounded by a ring of blackened vine ends. Their growing tips had been chewed off by the ants.

During his experiment, Janzen also noticed large areas of bare ground beneath older, ant-occupied acacias. Were these areas also cleared of other plants by the ants? To find out, Janzen planted seeds of three different plants in the bare ground. Worker ants carried some seeds away and they chewed off the stems of any seedlings that sprouted.

When he combined the data from all his plots, Janzen found that antless acacias grew far more slowly than ant-occupied acacias. During the wet season, the stems and branches of 433 antless acacias grew an average of just 1⅓ inches. In contrast, the stems and branches of 329 ant-occupied acacias grew an average of more than 38 inches—about 28 times more growth! Antless acacias also produced far fewer leaves, averaging 68 per stem as compared with 156 leaves per stem on ant-occupied plants. By the end of the year, a large number of antless acacias were dead due to insect or rodent damage, or because they were shaded out by vines or faster-growing trees.

The striking differences in the growth and survival of the two groups of bullhorn acacias proved that Thomas

Acacias with ants grew an average of 28 times faster than antless acacias.

Belt had been correct in 1874. Pseudomyrmex ants do ward off acacia leaf-eaters, both large and small. Just as important, they kill off plants that would otherwise crowd bullhorn acacias out of their places in the sun.

The ants aren't just helping the trees. They are also helping themselves. As a bullhorn acacia grows, it produces more nectar and protein to feed the ants and more thorns in which the ants can raise their young. *Pseudomyrmex* ants and bullhorn acacias clearly help each other survive and each has traits that specifically benefit the other.

Many kinds of tropical forest plants provide homes and special foods for certain kinds of ants that live in or on their stems. Scientists call all of these "ant-plants." Janzen's study showed that certain ants and ant-plants have a critically important, interdependent relationship. "Without their ant armies, bullhorn acacias would not be present in the dry tropical forests of Central America," he states. At the time of his study, Janzen pointed out that the mutual dependence of bullhorn acacias and *Pseudomyrmex* ants did not mean that all ant-plants depend upon their ants for survival. But as of 2002, he reports that, so far, additional studies of other ant and ant-plant species throughout the world have all revealed a similar interdependence.

TRICKSTERS
IN THE TREES

GIANT PASSIONVINE FLOWERS offer nectar to hummingbirds—and photo opportunities for any tourists lucky enough to chance upon them. Finding a passionvine in flower is not easy, even though hundreds of kinds of passionvines grow throughout Central and South America. The long stems of these plants wrap around tree trunks and creep through the treetops. But most species are uncommon, and each individual plant produces few flowers.

When they're not in bloom, these vines are even more difficult to see. Why are they so tricky to spot?

59

A hermit hummingbird visiting the large red flower of a passionvine.

A surprising answer was discovered by an unlikely detective, butterfly biologist Laurence Gilbert. At first, Gilbert wasn't interested in passionvines. He was studying *Heliconius* butterflies. Like passionvines, *Heliconius* butterflies are widespread throughout the tropics. They have long, dark wings, brightly marked with yellow, red, or orange spots or stripes. Their heads and eyes are among the largest of any butterfly species. In most tropical areas, many species of *Heliconius* butterflies live together—and most look similar. Nearly all species are poisonous to insect-eating predators. Their bright colors serve as a bold sign of their poisons, warning predators to leave them alone. So *Heliconius* butterflies have no need to hide, and they are easy to spot and follow around.

Gilbert became interested in *Heliconius* butterflies when he was just twelve years old. A vagrant *Heliconius* from the subtropics wandered into south Texas, where Gilbert lived. Awed by its size and beautiful markings, he wanted to catch it and add it to his collection, but the insect was in a public park. Gilbert's father did not allow

Like this one, most of the many species of Heliconius *butterflies are strikingly marked in black, yellow, and orange patterns.*

him to chase it down. Tantalized by the beauty of the butterfly that got away, Gilbert resorted to reading books about tropical butterflies. Years later, as an adult, he traveled to the tropics to study them.

Through hundreds of hours of field observations during the 1960s and early 1970s, Gilbert learned that these butterflies have many remarkable traits. He discovered that adult *Heliconius* eat both the nectar and the pollen from certain cucumber plants. The pollen provides the butterflies with extra nitrogen and other chemicals, which allows them to live longer and produce more eggs than other butterflies. Most butterflies live only a few weeks, but *Heliconius* live as long as six months. Females lay a few eggs each day throughout their adult lives.

Gilbert became interested in passionvines while following egg-laying female butterflies. Each species of *Heliconius* butterfly lays its eggs upon the new shoots of a particular species of passionvine, even though passionvine leaves are packed with toxic poisons that make them inedible to nearly all insects. *Heliconius* caterpillars are an exception. They devour and thrive on young passionvine leaves. In fact, Gilbert observed that passionvine plants are often ravaged by the caterpillars.

Young plants suffer the most. These plants get their start on the ground, springing up beneath small openings

A young passionvine has to grow quickly toward the sunlight and avoid being spotted by any egg-laying Heliconius *butterfly.*

in the forest canopy. In these openings, created when a tree falls or some overhead branches break off, enough sunlight reaches the forest floor to nourish new plants. But only the fastest-growing plants survive, because those that grow too slowly are soon shaded out. Gilbert noticed that just one *Heliconius* caterpillar munching on a young passionvine's leaves could prevent the plant from growing fast enough to stay in the sunlight. Trapped in the shade, a young plant can't mature.

Older passionvines have some protection from *Heliconius* caterpillars. Once the vines reach the treetops, most develop special glands on their stems or leaves that produce sugary sap. A wide variety of ants, wasps, and bees come to feed on this nectar. During their visits, they also attack and kill most *Heliconius* eggs

Heliconius *caterpillars devour passionvine leaves.*

and caterpillars. However, the few caterpillars that survive do significant damage. They graze off new leaves, often limiting a vine's growth and preventing it from storing up enough energy to produce flowers and seeds. Gilbert now suspects that part of the reason passionvines produce few flowers is because of the leaf damage inflicted by *Heliconius* caterpillars.

After many years, Gilbert realized that the best way to spot passionvines without flowers is to follow a female *Heliconius* butterfly. "I look for a *Heliconius* female and watch her," he says. "Soon she'll flit up to a vine that was right there in my view the whole time." Other researchers had reported that *Heliconius* use smell to find the general vicinity of their food plants, but Gilbert gathered evidence that they also use their eyes. He noticed that some *Heliconius* females mistakenly approached and landed on plants with leaf shapes similar to those of the passionvine species they laid eggs upon. Inspecting any plant other than a passionvine is a waste of time for a *Heliconius,* because its caterpillars can only eat passionvine leaves. Curious about the females' "mistakes," Gilbert began to study the shapes of passionvine leaves.

A Heliconius butterfly uses smell and vision to seek out an egg-laying site on passionvine leaves

The scientist traveled to Trinidad, Mexico, and Costa Rica and other parts of Central America. He collected young and old leaves from all the passionvines he could find in each forest he visited. Many tropical tree species have very simple oval leaves with a single long tip. In fact, this leaf shape is so widespread that tree identification in the tropics is exceedingly difficult for anyone but an expert. So Gilbert was surprised to discover tremendous variation in passionvine leaf shapes. A few species had simple leaves with long tips, but others had leaves divided into two, three, five, or eight lobes. There were passionvines with leaves that looked like those from maple, philodendron, ivy, and pepper plants.

To figure out why the leaf shapes varied so widely, Gilbert looked for patterns. He was surprised to note that only ten or fewer species of passionvine were present in most places he visited, although more than five hundred species of passionvines exist in the tropical regions of Mexico, Central America, and South America. Curiously,

At each location he visited, Gilbert found that those passionvine species present had surprisingly varied leaf shapes. The top row shows the passionvine leaf shapes he found at Turrialba, Costa Rica, while the lower row shows the leaf shape variety found in the Arima Valley on Trinidad.

each of the passionvine species present in any one area had mature leaves that differed in shape from their young leaves. And each of the species present had both young and old leaves of a shape unique among passionvine species in the same area. Why would a single passionvine species develop two different leaf shapes as it grew? And why did all the species of passionvines in each area look different from one another?

Gilbert found an important clue when he noticed a remarkable similarity between the leaves of some passionvines and the leaves of common tropical plants growing in the same area. He realized that he could find passionvines by looking around to note the leaf shape of the most common plant in a particular forest, then searching for a vine with the same leaf shape. Young passionvines often had leaves resembling those of common plants that grew near the ground. But these same plants, once mature, produced leaves that looked like those of common plants high in the forest canopy. Why would passionvines grow leaves that made them resemble common plants? Each question was leading to another.

As Gilbert thought about his observations, a surprising explanation occurred to him. Perhaps passionvines were mimicking common plants in order to trick or hide from *Heliconius* butterflies! Many kinds of animals use

Gilbert noticed this passionvine (Passiflora cuneata) produces long narrow leaves when it is a young plant, and broad, lobed leaves when it reaches the canopy. In both locations, the vine's leaves resemble those of other more common plant species (shown in lighter shading here).

camouflaging colors and shapes to hide from predators. Tropical forests are packed with moths, beetles, bugs, and even birds that look like dead leaves or tree bark. There are frogs and birds that look like green leaves, and spiders and wasps that look like flowers. So Gilbert's idea made sense.

The scientist reasoned that passionvines resembling common forest plants are probably more difficult for *Heliconius* females to locate because the butterflies seem to rely on leaf shape when they search for places to lay their eggs. Any plant with traits that prevent or delay *Heliconius* females from detecting its young shoots has a better chance of surviving and growing large enough to produce flowers and seeds. This idea would also explain why different passionvine species growing in the same area have different leaf shapes. Any passionvine species with a leaf shape similar to an already-established species is more likely to be spotted by female *Heliconius*, because the butterflies have already learned to seek out that leaf shape. To say it another way, the only seedling passionvines likely to survive are those with a leaf shape different from others in the area. Over time, such differences in the survival and seed production of passionvines would produce the leaf shape variations that Gilbert documented.

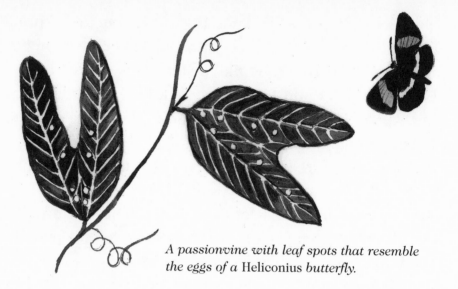

A passionvine with leaf spots that resemble the eggs of a Heliconius *butterfly.*

Gilbert discovered that some passionvine species have yet another trick up their leaves. He noticed that the new leaves of a few species were marked with tiny yellow dots. To his trained eye, these dots uncannily resembled the bright yellow eggs of a *Heliconius* butterfly. Why might a leaf have such yellow markings? Gilbert reviewed the facts. Before laying an egg, a female *Heliconius* flutters slowly around a passionvine. She alights here and there on various shoots, drums the leaves with her feet, and inspects the plant carefully. If she detects the presence of any *Heliconius* eggs, she moves to another shoot or plant instead of laying her egg. As a result, individual passionvine shoots rarely contain more than a single *Heliconius* egg. A female's search for other eggs is important, because *Heliconius* caterpillars eat each other. If a caterpillar hatches out on a leaf already occupied by a caterpillar, it will get eaten.

This information led Gilbert to suspect that the yellow leaf dots served as imitation butterfly eggs. He guessed that the vines with these dots might be tricking *Heliconius* butterflies into laying their eggs elsewhere. In the late 1970s, Gilbert enlisted the help of graduate biology student Kathy Williams to confirm his field observations with a laboratory experiment. In a greenhouse, the researchers offered captive *Heliconius* females a variety of passionvine shoots as places for egg-laying. Some shoots had no eggs or dots, some had *Heliconius* eggs, and some had the yellow dots that Gilbert calls "egg mimics." As the scientist

expected, the *Heliconius* females laid few eggs on the passionvine shoots with real yellow eggs. They also laid few eggs on shoots that displayed the yellow dots. Instead, they laid nearly all of their eggs on the shoots with no eggs or dots. This experiment confirmed Gilbert's idea that some passionvine species trick *Heliconius* females into avoiding their shoots.

Plants that hide from and trick their predators might seem like science fiction. But plants have developed many means of defending themselves from leaf-eating animals, including thorns, spines, sticky hairs, and a multitude of poisons. The use of camouflage and mimicry is not really so different.

After Gilbert published his findings, scientists found other plant species with leaf shapes and markings that seem to help them avoid detection by insect predators. Surprisingly, the list now includes plants that grow in temperate regions.

Many tight interconnections, like those between *Heliconius* butterflies and passionvines, exist in tropical forests because these forests contain so many highly specialized species. As scientists like Gilbert unravel the complex interrelationships in tropical forests, their findings may help us better understand how nature works throughout the world.

A Choco hunter uses a blowgun with darts dipped in the deadly poison taken from the skin of one kind of "poison-dart frog," Phyllobates terriblis.

THE SEARCH
FOR A DEADLY
FROG'S POISONS

MANY TROPICAL FROGS with bright red, yellow, and iridescent spots and stripes are protected by bitter-tasting chemicals on their skin. Any predator that catches one quickly spits it out. Frog-eating snakes, toads, birds, and even some large, predatory spiders learn to leave brightly colored frogs alone.

Yet in Colombia, the Choco people seek out three species of the brightly colored frogs. These particular frogs, sometimes called poison-dart or poison-arrow frogs, have chemicals on their skin that are more than just bitter-tasting. They are also deadly poisons. Even a drop of poison from the most deadly of these species, the terrible dart frog *(Phyllobates terriblis)*, can kill a human being. The Choco people rub their blowgun darts across the frogs' skins, using leaves to keep the poisons off their hands. They use the poison darts to kill the birds and animals they need for food.

John Daly, a scientist working with the U.S. National Institutes of Health, wanted to find out the exact chemical composition of the dart frogs' deadly poisons. He and others suspected that the frogs' poison chemicals might have value in medical research. Daly collected poison frogs in the tropical forests of Colombia in 1964, then returned to his lab in the United States, where he analyzed the frogs' skins. He discovered that the skins contained a kind of alkaloid,

or nitrogen-based molecule. Drugs like cocaine, morphine, and caffeine are examples of alkaloid chemicals. But the type of alkaloid Daly found in the terrible dart frog was new to science.

Charles Myers, a graduate student studying amphibians and reptiles in Panama, was intrigued by Daly's findings. He asked Daly to help him look at the poisons in other species of brightly colored tropical frogs. In the end, these two scientists worked together for over thirty years, collecting frogs of many species from all over Central and South America.

By analyzing the skins of so many tropical frogs, Daly discovered hundreds of new kinds of alkaloid chemicals. Most are bitter but far less toxic than those from the poison-dart frogs of Colombia. Daly was not surprised to find that different species of tropical frogs produced different poisons. But he was amazed to discover that frogs of the same species, when collected from different areas, often produced quite different poisons.

In hopes of learning more about the poisons, Daly and fellow scientists began keeping tropical frogs in terrariums during the 1970s. They fed the frogs fruit flies, crickets, and other insects easily raised in the laboratory. But a curious problem arose. Adult frogs kept in captivity gradually became less poisonous.

When kept in terrariums, these tropical frogs stopped producing poisons.

And frogs that were collected in the wild as eggs or tadpoles then raised in captivity never produced any poisons whatsoever.

At first, Daly suspected that something was wrong with the laboratory environment. He and his coworkers changed the lighting in the terrariums. They changed the temperature and the humidity. Still, these dart frogs remained nonpoisonous. Perhaps the frogs didn't produce poisons because life in the lab was too easy for them, Daly thought. To find out whether this was the case, the researchers threatened the frogs with a rotating black brush that resembled an attacking snake and placed live snakes in adjacent aquariums. The researchers also repeatedly moved the frogs from one terrarium to another. Despite these stresses, the captive frogs did not manufacture poisons.

Daly began to suspect that the frogs did not actually produce their poisons, but instead must somehow get them from their natural environment. To find out if frogs could concentrate poisons from something they ate, he and coworkers fed the frogs some fruit flies dusted with a powder that contained alkaloids. Some of the same alkaloids soon appeared in the frogs' skin glands. The test proved that the frogs could concentrate poisons from their food. Yet most of the alkaloids in the wild frogs' skins had never been found in nature. So where were the rain-forest frogs getting their poisons?

Daly unearthed a clue during the early 1990s when he examined some frogs sent to him by researchers in

Dendrobates auratus

Hawaii. Frogs from Panama had been released in Hawaii in 1932 and had established a wild population there. When Daly examined the wild Hawaiian frogs, he discovered that their skins contained very different poisons than the skins of their Panamanian relatives. Later he analyzed the skins of some captive-raised Hawaiian frogs. These frogs contained small amounts of the same poisons as the wild Hawaiian frogs. Once again, Daly was puzzled. Why did these captive-raised Hawaiian frogs contain poisons, when other captive tropical frogs did not?

Daly soon learned that the captive Hawaiian frogs had been fed a diet consisting mainly of insects caught in the Hawaiian forest. This information suggested that poison frogs must get some of their poisons from eating "wild" insects or other small invertebrates.

Daly wanted to know exactly which animals might be the source of the frogs' poisons. To find out, he and several coworkers in Panama raised dart frog tadpoles on two different diets. They fed fruit flies raised in the lab to one group of frogs. These frogs never produced any poisons. They fed ants, beetles, springtails, millipedes, and other invertebrates collected from the surrounding tropical forest to a second group of frogs. These frogs soon produced some, though not all, of the alkaloids found in wild frogs from the same area of Panama.

Daly and his coworkers next analyzed the various invertebrates they had collected to find out which ones might be the source of the frogs' poisons. They discovered a few frog poisons in certain species of the ants, beetles, and millipedes they had collected. This finding proved that at least some of the alkaloids of poison frogs come from invertebrates in their diet.

Daly and other scientists are still searching for sources of tropical frog poisons. To date, only about twenty of the five hundred alkaloids Daly discovered in frogs have been found in tropical insects or other invertebrates. Some studies suggest that many rainforest frogs feed mainly on ants, so Daly believes

researchers will find more frog poisons in ants. But he points out that the sources of hundreds of frog poisons, including the most toxic ones, remain a mystery. Some may originate from invertebrate species that haven't even been discovered yet.

Daly also wonders whether the invertebrates that contain frog toxins produce these poisons or get them from something they eat. Studies so far show that certain beetles and ants do make the frog poisons they contain. But Daly suspects that some of the hundreds of poison chemicals found in frog skins may be passed up through tropical forest food chains. Perhaps some are passed from plants to insects to frogs.

Daly's finding that frogs of a single species but from different forest areas contain different poisons is remarkable. His discovery that the frogs get many, if not all, of their poisons from the invertebrates they eat suggests that every patch of tropical forest could yield a treasure-trove of unknown chemicals and undiscovered creatures. "Each small part of the tropical forest," Daly says, "may be unique in terms of the creatures that occur there."

THE CURIOUS CASE OF THE HELPFUL PARASITES

MOST BIRDS BUILD their nests in secret places, well apart from the nests of other birds. They hide them to make it more difficult for predators and parasites to find their eggs and young. Because tropical forests harbor an especially large number and variety of nest predators and parasites, tropical bird nests are destroyed more often than nests in other environments. In fact, few hatchlings survive to leave their nests.

In spite of the dangers, some tropical birds do not hide their nests. Among these are two species that often place their individual nests together in a single tree: yellow-rumped caciques and chestnut-headed oropendolas. These black, robin-to-crow sized birds with flashy yellow markings are quickly spotted by most visitors to Central America or northern South America. They stand out because 10 to 150 of them typically build their large, hanging nests of woven grass together in a single tree. The highly visible nests seem an easy target, yet both species remain common. Why aren't their eggs and young quickly killed by predators and parasites?

Neal Smith, a researcher with the Smithsonian Tropical Research Institute, decided to investigate. He located 47 colonies of caciques and oropendolas along the Panama Canal. These colonies contained 1,750 individual nests in all. From 1964 to 1968, Smith visited the colonies at regular intervals throughout the nesting season. Before disturbing the nests, he took notes on the behavior of the birds. Then he used a ladder and telescoping aluminum poles to take down each nest for examination. He recorded the nest contents, then used tape and glue to return each nest to its original location.

Smith identified two types of nesting colonies established by caciques and oropendolas—wasp-tree colonies and waspless colonies. The wasp-tree colonies were located in trees that contained stinging ants and large nests of either wasps or biting bees. The waspless colonies were built in trees with no ants, wasps, or bees.

Thirteen of the 47 bird colonies Smith studied were waspless. In these colonies, the birds placed their hanging nests on the tips of the smallest branches, far from the tree trunk. Opossums, snakes, toucans, owls, and other predators cannot climb onto these thin branches, so few nests were lost to predators. However, the nests suffered greatly from two kinds of parasites—botflies and giant cowbirds.

Thirty-four of the nesting colonies Smith studied were built in wasp-trees. The insects attacked anything that disturbed their tree, even in total darkness. Despite hot, muggy weather, Smith had to wear long-sleeved shirts, long pants, gloves, and a headnet to avoid getting stung or bitten by the insects that swarmed out when he examined the nests. So even though nests in these colonies were suspended from sturdier branches, Smith was not surprised to find that few nests were destroyed by predators. Any predator unlucky enough to visit one of these trees no doubt left quickly.

On the other hand, Smith was puzzled to discover that nests in the wasp-tree colonies were rarely infested

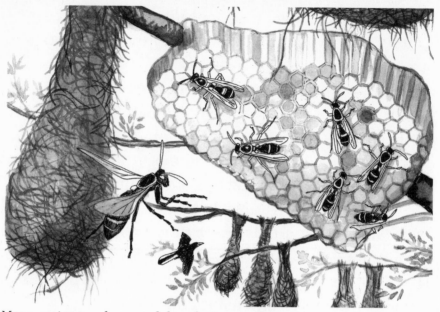

Many cacique and oropendola colonies are located in trees that contain nests of wasps or other stinging or biting insects.

or destroyed by botflies or cowbirds. These parasites fly directly into the birds' nests and do not disturb the tree branches or the insect nests. Thus, the stinging insects do not swarm out to attack as they do when large predators visit the tree. Smith figured the stinging insects ought to ignore these parasites just as they ignore the nesting birds. Yet his data suggested otherwise. How and why might stinging insects drive away botflies and cowbirds, he wondered.

Smith considered the botflies first. Botflies place their eggs or larvae on other animals. The wormlike larvae burrow into a host animal's body and grow by feeding on its tissues. Once the botfly larvae mature, they crawl out of the animal, then pass through a pupal stage before changing into their adult form. Different kinds of botflies parasitize different kinds of animals.

Smith hung flypaper in each of the colonies to trap adult botflies. He also carefully recorded the presence of botfly larvae on chicks and pupae in the nests. He discovered a clear pattern. Few botflies were present around the wasp-tree colonies, but he caught many botflies in the trees without wasps. Cacique and oropendola chicks can survive a few botfly larvae, but any chick infested with seven or more usually dies. Smith found that few chicks died from botfly infestation in the wasp-tree colonies, while many chicks died in the waspless colonies.

Smith's findings indicated that wasps and bees protect nesting caciques and oropendolas from parasitic botflies. The researcher reasoned that the stinging insects do not distinguish between botflies that parasitize birds and botflies that parasitize insects. Apparently, they attack and drive away all species of botfly invaders.

Next, Smith considered the giant cowbirds. He observed that the wasps and bees ignore cowbirds,

In wasp-tree colonies, caciques and oropendolas chased cowbirds (all-black bird above) away.

just as they ignore nesting caciques and oropendolas. There had to be some other explanation for the scarcity of cowbird parasites in wasp-protected colonies.

Smith considered the facts. Rather than building their own nests, cowbirds lay their eggs in the nests of other birds. The host birds incubate these eggs and eventually raise the cowbird young, apparently mistaking the chicks for their own offspring. Caciques and oropendolas are among the giant cowbird's hosts.

Because giant cowbird young hatch earlier and are larger than cacique and oropendola chicks, they eat much of the food brought back to the nests by the parent birds. Consequently, some host chicks starve to death when one or more cowbird chicks share their nest.

Smith noted that giant cowbirds visited nests in both types of colonies. However, the cowbirds received different receptions in the two colony types. In wasp-tree colonies, the caciques and oropendolas chased the cowbirds away, mobbing them and scolding them with loud squawks. Rejected cowbird eggs often littered the ground beneath these colonies. Not

surprisingly, Smith found that few cowbird young fledged from nests in wasp-protected trees. But those few nests parasitized by cowbirds produced only about half as many cacique and ororopendola young as nests without these parasites.

In the colonies without wasps, caciques and oropendolas rarely chased cowbirds away. They seldom rejected cowbird eggs, and plenty of cowbird chicks fledged from nests in these colonies. It seemed as if the birds in waspless colonies were allowing cowbirds to parasitize their nests. What could explain this strange behavior?

Smith found a good explanation by carefully examining his four years of nesting records. In waspless colonies, cacique and oropendola chicks in many nests suffered infestations of botflies and died. The exceptions were those chicks who shared their nest with one or two cowbird chicks. These young were usually free of botflies, and many survived.

Why the higher survival rates? Smith observed that young cowbirds help their nestmates by picking off and eating botfly larvae. Overall, in waspless colonies, three times more cacique and oropendola chicks fledged from nests containing cowbird young than from nests without cowbirds. This was just the opposite of the situation in wasp-protected colonies.

Smith observed that young cowbirds help their nestmates by picking off and eating botfly larvae.

The researcher concluded that, in waspless colonies, cowbird parasites are more helpful than harmful to the caciques and oropendolas. This probably explains the less hostile reception that cowbirds receive at these colonies.

In most years, caciques and oropendolas nesting in wasp-tree colonies produce the most young. But these birds cannot nest until the stinging insects also begin nesting, which occurs late in the dry season. If the wet season begins early, the late nesters lose their young in the rains. As a result, colonies in waspless trees actually produce more young in wet years.

Smith also noted that wasps and bees sometimes abandon their nests for no apparent reason. This leaves previously wasp-protected colonies vulnerable to both predators and parasites, and most of the vulnerable nests fail. In addition, caciques and oropendolas in wasp-trees can nest only once each year—when the stinging insects are nesting. Birds nesting in waspless trees can nest two to three times each year. Smith suspects that these factors and others ensure that both types of colonies—and both types of behavior—survive.

Smith's study reveals that nature is surprisingly variable. Animals can behave differently under different circumstances. And seemingly harmful parasites can sometimes help their hosts survive.

THE BUTTERFLIES' STRANGE PURSUIT

ONE AFTERNOON in 1978, biologist Tom Ray wanted a break from his study of tropical vines at Finca La Selva, Costa Rica, so he took a walk in the forest. When he stumbled across an army ant swarm, he stopped to watch one of the more fascinating scenes in nature.

Army ants can't kill anything larger than a mouse or a small lizard, but their bites and stings are painful to humans. Ray tucked his pants legs into his socks and stepped carefully as a drama unfolded.

Where moments before the dim forest floor seemed deserted in the hot stillness of midday, it now teemed with life. Several columns of black ants flowed outward in many directions from the main swarm. Marching over the damp, dead leaves on the forest floor, the tiny predators bit and stung to death any prey unlucky enough to be caught. Just ahead of the advancing ant swarm, beetles, bugs, flies, centipedes, and other invertebrates crawled, hopped, and flew out of hiding in an attempt to escape the invading army.

A moment later, the forest was alive with the whir of wings and the snap of bills, as a legion of birds emerged to feast on the fleeing insects. Snap! Ray watched as an antbird caught an escaping grasshopper. Click! He saw a leafhopper meet its end in the bill of a woodcreeper.

Another day, watching and identifying the ant-following birds might have engaged all of Ray's attention, but today he happened to notice something else. Several tiger-striped, yellow, black, and orange butterflies were flitting around above the ants. They dipped down and landed in and around the swarming ants—a behavior that struck Ray as dangerous.

He watched closely to see whether any butterflies were killed by the army ants. He did not see any that were captured. When a butterfly lit near him, Ray

A variety of antbirds and other bird species follow army ant swarms to feast on the insects that the army ants scare out of hidding.

noticed that it landed momentarily on a white spot. He watched other individuals. Each butterfly alighted on a different white spot. Most of the spots appeared to be bird droppings.

Ray suspected that he had just discovered a curious connection between army ants, ant-following birds, and these butterflies. But to find out if his idea was right, he needed more information.

He first consulted butterfly expert Bob Silverglade. Silverglade identified the tiger-striped butterflies as members of the Ithomiinae butterfly family. This group of long-winged butterflies includes many species whose caterpillars feed on poisonous plants of the nightshade family. The caterpillars store the nightshade poisons in their bodies, which makes them poisonous as adults. Birds and mammals recognize the adult butterflies' bright wing markings as a warning that these insects are poisonous and don't pursue them. So these butterflies don't need to hide and are often seen flitting around tropical forests. Yet Ray had never seen so many in one place.

The biologist searched the scientific literature to find out what other scientists knew about the behavior of ithomiine butterflies around army ants. Butterfly biologist B. A. Drummond had reported their odd, dipping flight around army ant swarms in 1976. He had also noted the pungent odor of the pheromones produced by the ants. Pheromones are smelly chemicals that many animals make to attract or locate mates, or to communicate other information. Noting that all the ithomiine butterflies he saw around army ants were females, Drummond suggested that the female butterflies confused the smell of the ants with the scent produced by male ithomiine butterflies.

But in 1978 another butterfly biologist, W. A. Haber, determined that the mating pheromone produced by ithomiine butterflies attracts both males and females. So Ray discarded Drummond's idea.

An immaculate antbird snatches a caterpillar scared from its hiding place by army ants.

A. M. Young, another butterfly biologist, had proposed a different explanation. He thought female ithomiine butterflies might be attracted to ant swarms by the odor of decay that surrounds the killing swarm. Young argued that this smell might attract ithomiines because these butterflies sometimes feed on juices from decaying fruits and animal carcasses.

After studying the literature, Ray enlisted fellow biologist Catherine Andrews to help him gather more field observations. Over the next year, the two scientists tracked down thirteen active army ant swarms so they could observe and capture ithomiines in the vicinity of each swarm. They also observed and captured ithomiines from the same forest areas on days when the army ants were not present. They recorded the behavior of each butterfly they observed, then captured it to determine its sex.

On average, the scientists captured five ithomiines per hour around ant swarms, but less than one ithomiine per hour when the ants were absent. They sometimes saw eight to twelve butterflies flitting around a single ant swarm, and they captured more than thirty butterflies in just a few hours around one swarm. These observations proved that ithomiines are attracted to ant swarms.

Around the swarms, female ithomiines outnumbered males by ten to one. In contrast, the clusters of ithomiine

*Ithomiine butterflies swarm
around army ants.*

butterflies away from ant swarms contained far more male than female butterflies. This information confirmed Drummond's original observation that the ithomiines gathered around ant swarms are mostly females.

Ray and Andrews's records of butterfly behavior showed that over half of the individual butterflies observed around ant swarms had landed on white spots. Some of the spots were lichens or bits of fungi that resembled bird droppings, but most were wet bird droppings, just as Ray had suspected. Why would female butterflies land on bird droppings? Ray learned the answer from Bob Silverglade.

Butterflies feed mainly on flower nectar. Nectar is full of sugars, but it usually contains little or no nitrogen. Female butterflies require a lot of nitrogen to form their eggs. They store some in their bodies when they feed on leaves as caterpillars, but ithomiines are unusual in that they live for four months or longer. They cannot produce eggs throughout their adult lives unless they obtain additional nitrogen. Silverglade explained that because butterflies have mouths that work like straws, there are few nitrogen-rich things they can eat. Female ithomiines get the nitrogen they need by sipping the nitrogen-rich fluids in fresh bird droppings.

Because it is difficult to even see a bird in the dense foliage of a tropical forest, ithomiines must have a tough time finding fresh bird droppings. But dozens of ant-following birds accompany every swarm of army ants. As these birds feast on insects fleeing from the ants, they also deposit their droppings. Considering the female ithomiines' need for fresh bird droppings, Ray and Andrews figured that it made sense for the females to congregate around army ant swarms.

Because butterflies have a good sense of smell and rely heavily on scents to locate food and mates, Ray and Andrews concluded that female ithomiines most likely home in first on the pungent pheromones given off by the swarming army ants. Then they probably use vision and smell to locate the fresh bird droppings.

The ithomiine butterflies' strange relationship with army ants and the birds that follow them is an example of the complicated connections that exist among tropical forest creatures. It also reveals one curious way in which a tropical forest's limited nutrients are quickly and efficiently recycled.

An ithomiine butterfly sipping up nutrients from a bird dropping.

THE CASE OF THE WINGED FRUIT THIEVES

WHILE WORKING in the tropical rain forest of La Selva, Costa Rica, during the early 1970s, researcher Henry Howe watched toucans, flycatchers, parrots, and other birds feasting on the ripe fruits of a cerillo tree. His observations led him to suspect a theft was in progress.

Scientists think plants grow tasty fruits as a way of enticing animals to carry their seeds to new locations. However, not all fruit-eating animals transport the seeds. Some are "fruit thieves." They eat the fruits, but they don't carry the seeds anywhere. Howe noticed that many of the tropical birds were eating cerillo fruits but dropping the seeds right beneath the parent trees.

Did that matter? Howe thought that it might matter a great deal. The scattered distribution of most tropical tree species indicates that seeds dropped under or near a parent tree rarely grow into mature trees. While a twenty-five-acre plot of rain forest may contain hundreds of species of trees, most species are represented by no more than a few individual trees. And these individuals usually grow far from one another.

Scientists reason that this may be because piles of fallen seeds and fruit under a parent tree are likely to attract many seed-eating insects and small mammals. If so, few seeds would survive to grow. Also, most seedling trees have less chance of surviving in the shade of a parent tree than in another site where the forest canopy is more open. A tree species survives in the forest only if its seeds and seedlings escape predators, parasites, and diseases long enough to grow into new adult trees. If few or no seeds survive, the species will disappear when all the older trees die.

As Howe watched the birds feeding in the cerillo tree, he considered the tree's importance to the La Selva rain forest. Fruit-eating animals there face a food shortage at the end of the wet season in December and January because few trees bear fruit at that time. The cerillo tree is an exception. Its marble-sized fruits ripen during this period. Each fruit has a hard husk that splits open to reveal a cream-colored seed wrapped in a red-orange fleshy structure called an aril. Because few other foods are available, fruit-eating birds flock around cerillo trees to feast on the energy-rich arils. Many of the birds probably would not survive this season without cerillo trees.

Because the continued survival of cerillo trees is important to so many bird species, Howe decided to find out exactly what happened to cerillo seeds that were dropped directly beneath the parent trees. He collected and examined hundreds of seeds, looking for the telltale holes left by insect predators. Only a small portion of the seeds were injured by weevils, bark beetles, or other insects. Howe also attempted to feed cerillo seeds to various small mammals that live in the area. Most would not eat the seeds, but two small mice that did eat them soon died in convulsions. He concluded that cerillo seeds contain poisons. This unexpected finding suggested that most seeds dropped beneath a parent cerillo tree do survive.

Next, Howe watched to see how many of the cerillo seeds dropped under parent trees grew into trees. In February, thousands of seedlings sprouted up beneath the parent trees. By the following October, however, all of the seedlings were gone. Howe suspects they were eaten by agoutis—small, rabbit-like rodents

Howe suspected that agoutis ate the thousands of seedlings that sprouted up beneath the cerillo trees.

that are abundant in the rain forests of Costa Rica. Though captive agoutis won't eat cerillo seeds, they readily eat the seedlings. Whatever the cause, the cerillo seedlings had not survived. This showed that dropping cerillo seeds beneath a parent tree amounts to fruit thievery.

But which of the many fruit-eating birds were thieves? To find out, Howe studied sixteen cerillo trees in the La Selva rain forest during the fruiting season of December and January. He visited each tree with ripe fruit during late morning or late afternoon, when most birds feed. He made a total of 658 tree visits during the fruiting season. On each visit, he recorded both the number and kinds of birds present and made careful notes on the feeding behavior of each species.

Howe observed a total of twenty-two bird species feeding on cerillo fruits. These included two kinds of parrots, two kinds of toucans, an araceri, a wood-pecker, several kinds of flycatchers, and several kinds of cotingas, including the masked tityra.

Howe noted that different bird species ate the fruits in different ways. Amazon parrots perched on the tree branches, then used their strong beaks to strip the edible part of the fruit off the seeds. They immediately dropped the inedible seeds beneath the parent tree.

Social Flycatcher

Parrots stripped the edible portion of the fruit, then dropped the seeds beneath the parent tree.

Gray-capped and social flycatchers ate one fruit every two to three minutes, then rested for up to fifteen minutes. Before eating again, they spit out the hard seeds. Since the resting flycatchers almost always perched in the tree where they were feeding, nearly all the seeds they ate dropped under the parent tree. Toucans typically landed in a cerillo tree and fed on its fruits for a long time. They also spit out most seeds

110

Toucans ate the edible part of the fruits and dropped the seeds under the trees.

while perched in the tree. All of these birds were eating cerillo fruits but spreading very few of the seeds.

Only one bird species regularly carried cerillo seeds elsewhere—the masked tityra. These white, robin-sized birds are quiet and secretive. They are easy to overlook in a tree filled with noisy parrots and brightly colored toucans and araceris. Howe had to watch carefully to spot them and record their behavior. Through many observations, he noted that the tityras usually stayed in a cerillo tree for less than two minutes—long enough to pluck and gobble down one to ten cerillo fruits. Then the birds flew off to perch in some other tree. Howe never saw tityras spit out seeds while they were feeding on or perched in a cerillo tree. However, he was able to recover some seeds they spit out while sitting in other trees. Due to the manner in which they feed, Howe estimated that masked tityras must carry away at least three times more cerillo seeds per visit than any other bird species.

The pattern of tree visits also varied among bird species. Howe found that most birds fed in the cerillo trees in the morning only, and during only part of the fruiting season. For example, toucans visited the trees often in December but rarely in January. Gray-capped and social flycatchers ate cerillo fruits only in January. Rufous mourners and black-cheeked wood-

Masked tityras gobbled down several whole cerillo fruits, then flew off to perch in other trees to finish eating and spit out the inedible seeds.

peckers visited the trees only in late January. The masked tityra was the only species that ate cerillo fruits throughout the day and visited the trees throughout the entire fruiting season. So it was the only species that carried away cerillo seeds throughout the entire fruiting season.

Based on his field study, Howe concluded that parrots, toucans, flycatchers, and most cotingas are fruit thieves in cerillo trees. They eat cerillo fruits but drop most of the seeds beneath the parent tree, where the seedlings cannot survive. Only masked tityras truly "earn their fruit" by carrying cerillo seeds off to sites where they may someday grow into adult trees.

Small, easily overlooked species like the masked

Only masked tityras "earn" their fruit by carrying many seeds away from the parent cerillo trees and depositing them in places where they have a chance to grow into new trees.

tityra may not seem important. But Howe's research shows that relatively obscure creatures sometimes play critical roles. By spreading cerillo seeds, tityras help ensure that these trees continue to grow in the forest, bearing fruit at a time of year when fruit-eating animals can find little else to eat. In the La Selva rain forest, all the birds, insects, and other animals that need cerillo trees—and the trees themselves—may depend on the continued existence and behavior of one small, easily overlooked bird species: the masked tityra.

THE MYSTERY
IN THE
MONKEY DUNG

MONKEY DUNG is not a subject that interests most people. But scientists Alejandro Estrada and Rosamond Coates-Estrada became fascinated with this topic while studying the feeding habits of howling monkeys in the Los Tuxtlas forest of southern Mexico. In field observations made from 1983 to 1988, the Estradas discovered that howling monkeys ate many different kinds of fruit. Informed by the research of many other scientists, the Estradas knew that some fruit-eating animals play a critically important role in tropical forests by spreading the seeds of fruit-producing plants. They wondered whether the howling monkeys at Los Tuxtlas were dispersing seeds from the fruits they ate.

Monkeys disperse seeds mainly by ingesting them while eating fruit, then depositing the seeds in their droppings. So there was only one way for the Estradas to find the answer to their question. They had to get interested in monkey dung.

Collecting howler droppings was not an easy task. While observing the howling monkeys up in the treetops, the Estradas sometimes saw one of the animals defecate. Then they hurried to collect the fresh droppings that fell to the forest floor. Usually, however, the scientists could not see exactly where the droppings had landed, because tree trunks, branches, and vines obstructed their view. As a result, they often had to search to find the monkey dung. When they were successful, they placed each sample they located in a small plastic bag and carefully recorded the location where it was collected.

The Estradas spent many months collecting monkey droppings for analysis. Next, they removed the seeds from each dropping and identified the tree species from which each seed originated. By measuring the distance between the location where each dung-embedded seed was found and the nearest tree of the same species, the scientists were able to determine how far the monkeys had carried the seeds of different trees. Their findings indicated that howling monkeys carried the seeds of twenty-eight fruit tree species significant distances away from parent trees. In some cases, the monkeys carried seeds half a mile before depositing them.

However, not all seeds that pass through the digestive tract of an animal remain alive. Sometimes the seeds get crushed or partially digested, so they cannot grow. The Estradas wanted to find out whether the seeds in monkey droppings could grow into new plants. To do this, they planted sample seeds from the monkey droppings and other seeds collected directly from the various fruit trees.

Over four-fifths of the seeds taken from monkey droppings sprouted within a few months after being

Seeds from monkey-droppings sprouted quickly.

planted in canisters of soil. Many germinated more quickly than similarly planted seeds taken from uneaten fruits. These findings strongly suggested that howling monkeys are important seed carriers for twenty-eight fruit tree species at Los Tuxtlas.

However, the Estradas had noticed something that made them wonder whether seeds in monkey droppings survive to grow in the wild. They noted that monkey dung collected as soon as it hit the ground usually contained many seeds. But dung samples collected a few hours or even several minutes after they landed often contained few seeds or none at all. It seemed to the researchers that the number of seeds found in monkey droppings depended on how long the droppings had lain on the forest floor.

Curious to see if their impression was correct, the Estradas placed samples of monkey dung containing known numbers of seeds on the forest floor. They checked the samples later to see if any seeds had disappeared. After just twenty-four hours, most and sometimes all of the seeds had disappeared from every sample. What was causing the seeds to disappear?

Other scientists had reported that small rodents often eat seeds out of animal droppings. When the Estradas searched carefully, they found remnants of some of the missing seeds near some dung samples.

Small rodents seek out and eat the seeds embedded in howling monkey droppings

Suspicious scrapings left by small, sharp teeth indicated that these seeds had been eaten by small rodents. Hoping to discover which rodents were the culprits, the Estradas set out small live traps baited with seeds. The traps soon yielded two kinds of seed-eating mammals—spiny pocket mice and white-footed deer mice.

If most or all of the seeds in monkey droppings were eaten by seed-eating mice, the seeds spread by howling monkeys might never survive to grow. And if this were true, the monkeys were not helping the fruit trees reproduce after all. But there were young fruit trees growing in the forest, so the Estradas reasoned

121

that at least a few of the seeds in monkey droppings must somehow escape getting eaten by mice. What could explain the survival of some seeds?

The scientists had an idea. While collecting droppings, they had encountered many dung beetles. These insects bury small balls or clumps of animal droppings, then lay their eggs on these droppings. The dung serves as food for dung beetle young when they hatch. Some dung beetle species, called burrowers, bury clumps of droppings in the ground right beneath the dung pile. Other species, called ball rollers, make up a ball of dung and roll it away, burying it elsewhere. Dung beetles don't eat seeds, but the Estradas wondered whether the beetles might accidentally bury some of the seeds embedded in monkey dung. They decided to learn more about dung beetles.

First the researchers placed dozens of open cans baited with monkey droppings out in the forest. Fifteen species of dung beetles soon wandered into these traps. The scientists were surprised to find that dung beetles often located the droppings less than one minute after they were set out. In a separate experiment, the scientists placed samples of monkey dung on the ground. They found that dung beetles relocated or buried these samples within two and one-half hours.

The scientists set up a separate experiment to figure out whether dung beetles buried seeds along with the monkey droppings. First they cleared several small areas on the forest floor. Then they placed a sample of monkey dung containing a known number of seeds at each site. At some sites, they placed the dung samples inside small cages made of wire mesh. The mesh would keep mice out, while allowing dung beetles in. At other sites, the dung samples were not caged, allowing access by both mice and beetles.

The Estradas examined all these samples twenty-four hours later. About two-fifths of the seeds from the monkey dung inside the cages had disappeared, while

Dung beetles often located monkey droppings less than one minute after the droppings were placed on the ground.

three-fifths of the seeds in the uncaged dung samples had disappeared. What had happened to all the seeds? The Estradas carefully dug up the soil under and around all the dung sample sites to determine whether any of the missing seeds had been buried by dung beetles. They found nearly all of the seeds missing from the mouse-proof cages in dung balls buried underneath or near the cages. But only about one-eighth of the seeds missing from the uncaged samples were buried nearby.

This experiment indicated to the Estradas that mice probably eat most of the seeds in monkey droppings, but some are buried by dung beetles. Because mice often dig up roots and seeds buried in the soil, the scientists were unsure whether seeds buried by dung beetles would escape detection by mice. They suspected that the answer depended on two factors— how deep the dung beetles bury the balls containing seeds, and how well the mice can locate buried seeds.

In their field experiment, the Estradas had found seeds in dung buried at depths ranging from less than one-half inch up to four inches. To obtain more measurements and confirm their field observations, the scientists captured a variety of dung beetles. They placed the beetles inside large canisters containing soil and monkey droppings with known numbers of embedded seeds. After each captive beetle buried dung, the researchers carefully excavated to determine exactly how deep the dung was buried and how many seeds were buried with it.

Based on their field observations and the behavior of these captive beetles, the Estradas confirmed that dung beetles at Los Tuxtlas bury seeds at depths of less than one-half inch up to four and one-half inches under the surface. They found that ball-rolling species of dung beetles buried fewer seeds at shallower depths than burrowing species. Both types of dung beetles buried small seeds more often than large seeds. All told, the captive beetles buried 689 of the 1,667 seeds

Captive dung beetles buried monkey droppings and some embedded seeds at depths of one-half to four and one-half inches.

in the monkey dung samples. Three-quarters of these seeds were buried at depths greater than one inch, about half at depths greater than two inches. Less than one-quarter of the buried seeds were placed at depths greater than three inches.

The Estradas didn't yet know whether mice could detect seeds buried at these depths. It wasn't possible to observe mice searching for seeds in the wild, so they decided to capture some mice and assess their ability to locate seeds buried in soil within an experimental box. The researchers built a large wooden box with a screened top and filled it with about eight inches of soil. They covered the soil with a layer of dead leaves from the forest floor and placed a small piece of plastic pipe in the box as a hiding spot for the mice.

In a series of nine similar experiments, the Estradas released one wild-caught mouse into the box and allowed it three days to get used to being there. Then, while the mouse was hiding inside the pipe, they removed the cage top and pushed a known number of seeds into the soil, burying them at varying depths. They also spread a known number of seeds on the soil surface. The next day, the scientists checked to see how many of the seeds had been located and eaten by the captive mouse. They repeated this experiment using two kinds of mice and six kinds of seeds.

Each time the Estradas repeated the experiment, the captive mouse located some but not all of the seeds. The most deeply buried seeds consistently escaped detection. Overall, the mice found and ate almost all of the seeds on the soil surface, slightly more than half of those buried at depths of one to two inches, less than one-sixth of those buried at depths between two and three inches, and only a very few of the seeds buried more than three inches below the surface. The researchers concluded that some of the seeds in buried monkey droppings probably escape detection by forest mice, allowing the seeds a chance to sprout and grow into new trees.

Other scientists have gathered much evidence demonstrating that very few of the thousands of seeds produced by any tropical fruit tree survive to grow. The Estradas' careful research suggests that the full story of seed survival is a complicated one. They believe that some of the tropical fruit tree species in the Los Tuxtlas forest need both howling monkeys and dung beetles to ensure that a few of their seeds survive to grow into new trees.

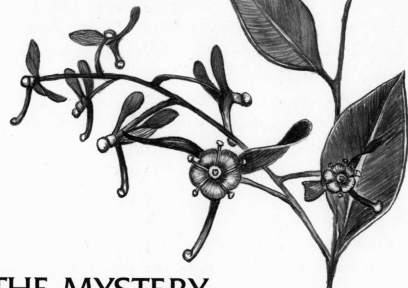

THE MYSTERY OF THE UNKNOWN POLLINATORS

SOUROUBEA GUIANENSIS is a sprawling, woody vine that climbs more than thirty feet into the treetops of low-land tropical forests. Researchers have named it, noted its occurrence in scattered locations in Central and South America, and stored samples of its leaves and flowers in museums. But until 1994, when flower biologists Isabel Machado and Ariadna Lopes became interested in it, no scientist had studied the vine carefully.

129

Machado and Lopes noticed *Souroubea*'s unusually shaped red and yellow flowers on vines growing in a four-square-mile tropical forest reserve in the city of Recife, Brazil. The scientists immediately wondered how the flowers were pollinated. Most flowering plants cannot produce seeds unless pollen from another plant of the same species is deposited on the stigmas, or female parts, of their flowers. Though some plants rely on wind to carry their pollen, most tropical forest plants depend upon insects, birds, or bats.

Machado and Lopes figured that this vine must be animal-pollinated, because plants that need animals as pollinators usually have large, colorful flowers. The scientists hoped to work up a "profile" of *Souroubea*'s pollinators based on the unique features of its flowers.

The true flowers of *Souroubea* are only about one-half inch in diameter with bright yellow petals. But each flower appears about one and three-quarters inches tall due to a large modified leaf called a bract, which grows alongside each small blossom. Two portions of this bright red-orange bract arch up from the flower like miniature wings, while a third portion extends downward. This downward portion forms a long narrow tube, or spur, which is filled with sugar-rich nectar. The vine's bright flowers grow in large clusters. Only one flower within each cluster opens during each day of the vine's flowering season, typically in late afternoon. The open bloom gives off a strong, sweet smell.

Visiting animals can pollinate a plant only if they contact the pollen-bearing stamens and pollen-receiving stigmas of its flowers. Considering the *Souroubea*'s flower structure, Machado and Lopes figured that only an animal with a long, narrow bill or tongue could reach into the deep spur to obtain the nectar while also bumping against the flower's reproductive parts. Among the animals that seemed capable of this feat, the scientists listed humming-birds, long-tongued bats, moths, butterflies, and other long-tongued insects.

The researchers narrowed their list of suspects based on the flower's bright red-orange color. Flowers pollinated by bats and moths are usually pale white or cream—colors that are more visible at night. Bees rarely pollinate red flowers because they can't see red. Birds or butterflies—animals that can see red—seemed most likely to be attracted by the bright red-orange bracts of *Souroubea* flowers.

Next, the researchers ruled out birds as likely pollinators of *Souroubea,* due to the strong, sweet smell of its flowers. Most birds have a poor sense of smell, and bird-pollinated flowers usually lack odors. In

Many kinds of animals, including perching birds (1), monkeys (2), bats (3), hummingbirds (4), beetles (5), bees (6), moths (7), and butterflies (8) are important pollinators. But each kind of pollinator generally visits only flowers of specific shapes, sizes, colors, smells, and/or nectar. The researchers used information about the types of flowers visited by each kind of animal to narrow down their suspect list.

132

contrast, flowers pollinated by bees, moths, and butter-flies often produce sweet-smelling perfumes that attract these scent-sensitive insects. Machado and Lopes decided that *Souroubea*'s pollinators were most likely long-tongued insects of some sort, probably butterflies.

The scientists wanted to find out if their hypothesis was correct, so they sat near blooming *Souroubea* vines in the Recife forest and watched carefully for animal visitors. They were able to observe some flowers close up and used binoculars to watch other flowers in the treetop vines. To be certain they did not miss any visitors, Machado and Lopes observed many *Souroubea* vines throughout the flowering season of three different years. They watched for flower visitors on several days during each flowering season, and during various hours of the day, ranging from 4:30 A.M. until midnight. The scientists spent a total of 105 hours observing the flowers—a far longer period of time than is generally needed to identify a plant's pollinators.

During their long hours of observation, Machado and Lopes saw only one kind of animal visit the *Souroubea* flowers. Surprisingly, it did not fit the pollinator profile they had carefully worked out. Instead of a butterfly or other long-tongued insect, the sole visitor to the flowers was a small hummingbird called the reddish hermit.

The researchers spent 105 hours observing the Souroubea *flowers and watching for any animal visitors.*

Machado and Lopes were puzzled. The clues did not add up. If a hummingbird was *Souroubea*'s only pollinator, why did the flowers have such a strong, sweet smell? The researchers speculated that the hermits might not be pollinators.

The most effective pollinators visit flowers mainly around the time they open, which is when the flowers contain the most nectar and are ready to receive or dispense pollen. Yet the hermits visited both open and unopened *Souroubea* flowers at all times of day, not just in the late afternoon when the flowers opened. The researchers also noticed that reddish hermits

Reddish hermits were the only flower visitors observed during the 105 hours the researchers spent watching Souroubea *vines.*

could not reach the bottom of the deep, nectar-filled spurs because their bills are too short. In addition, the birds almost always approached the flowers from the side rather than from the front. Thus these humming-birds rarely if ever contacted the flowers' pollen-bearing stamens or pollen-receiving stigmas while taking nectar. All these clues suggested that reddish hermits were probably nectar robbers—animals that take nectar but do not transfer pollen.

The scientists then wondered if *Souroubea* vines might be able to form seeds without receiving pollen from another plant. Some kinds of plants can self-pollinate, fertilizing their own eggs with pollen from their own flowers. Other kinds of plants do not require any pollen for seed development. Their eggs spontaneously develop into viable seeds through a process called apomixis. Both types of plants form seeds even when wind and all possible pollinators are kept away from the flowers.

The scientists needed to know more. They set up an experiment to determine whether *Souroubea* vines require a pollinator and, if so, whether reddish hermits are effective pollinators of its flowers. During two flowering seasons, the scientists tagged 186 unopened *Souroubea* flower buds on several different plants. These tagged buds were then left alone, so that

The researchers tagged and numbered 186 Souroubea *flowers. They excluded hermits and other flower visitors from another forty-nine flowers by tying mesh bags around flower clusters.*

reddish hermits or other animals could visit the flowers once they opened.

The researchers prevented hermits and other animals from reaching another forty-nine flowers by tying bags of fine nylon mesh around the unopened buds. Machado and Lopes left fourteen of the forty-nine buds in the bags during *Souroubea*'s entire flowering season to find out if any would self-pollinate. They ensured self-pollination in twenty-one of the forty-nine flowers by using a small paintbrush to carefully transfer pollen from the stamens to the stigma of each flower. To do this, they briefly removed, then replaced, the mesh bags. To test whether the flowers could set seed in the absence of pollen (through apomixis), the scientists briefly removed the bags from the remaining fourteen bagged buds, clipped off the stamens and pollen to prevent self-pollination, then replaced the bags.

At the end of the two flowering seasons, Machado and Lopes tallied how many flowers in each group had set seed. Their results were clear. None of the flowers that remained in the bags throughout either flowering season produced seeds. None of the flowers that the researchers had dusted with a paintbrush to ensure self-pollination produced seeds. And none of the flowers with removed stamens set seed. These results indicated that *Souroubea* flowers must receive pollen from another *Souroubea* plant in order to produce seeds.

Had the flowers left open to visits by reddish hermits been pollinated by this animal visitor? Again, the results were clear. Of the 186 tagged flowers accessible to hermits, only nine had produced seeds. Many more *Souroubea* flowers should have formed seeds if reddish hermits were effective pollen carriers.

Thus, the mystery of the unknown pollinators remains unsolved. Machado and Lopes still suspect that the true pollinators of *Souroubea* are some type of long-tongued insects, most likely butterflies. But after several years of observation, they no longer expect to find *Sourboubea's* pollinators in the Recife forest reserve. They point out that the Recife forest is one of the few remaining fragments of Brazil's Atlantic coast rain forest. Most of this once-vast forest had been cut down and cleared during the thirty years prior to their study. Due to the small size of the remaining forest fragments, many mammals, birds, and insects that once lived there have become rare, or have disappeared entirely. Machado and Lopes now think that the pollinators of *Souroubea* are among the species that have disappeared.

If the pollinators are gone, the long-term future for the *Souroubea* vine in the Recife forest patch does not look bright. The existing vines may continue to live and grow for a long time. But without an effective pollinator, their flowers will produce very few seeds. Consequently, it is unlikely that new *Souroubea* plants will grow to replace those that die.

When a species can no longer reproduce, its eventual extinction is certain, even if many individuals remain alive. Tropical biologists use the term "living dead" to describe such creatures. The living dead are plants and animals that still exist, but are likely doomed to extinction because the other living things they depend upon for survival or reproduction no longer exist in adequate numbers. Whether the *Souroubea* vines of Brazil's Atlantic forest should be added to a list of living-dead species there remains uncertain.

Fortunately, *Souroubea guianesis* also occurs in other Atlantic forest fragments, and in other parts of South and Central America. Machado and Lopes hope researchers in other places will take up the search for this plant's still-unknown pollinators. If the pollinators can be identified, it might be possible to bring them back to Recife. If not, *Souroubea* vines most likely will disappear gradually from that forest reserve.

Tropical forests are jam-packed with thousands of unique plant and animal species, many of which depend upon each other in remarkable ways. This is partly why biologists consider tropical forests fragile ecosystems. Just as the absence of a pollinator may lead to the disappearance of *Souroubea* vines, the loss of even a few species may have surprising and unpredictable effects upon the entire forest.

HOW MUCH FOREST IS ENOUGH?

OVER THE LAST thirty years, people have been destroying tropical forests at alarming rates. Humans are cutting trees to obtain wood and fuel, and clearing forests to create fields for raising crops and cattle. Some sources estimate that the tropical forests of Central and South America are disappearing at 26,500 square miles per year, or about three square miles per hour. If the destruction continues at current rates, most tropical forests will disappear during the first half of this century. Because tropical forests are home to over half of all the plant and animal species on Earth, scientists predict that a large portion of our planet's plant and animal life could disappear with them.

To avert such a catastrophe, many people have been working to set up tropical forest parks and nature reserves. They hope such reserves might save some of the thousands of species that make up tropical forest ecosystems. But how big does a tropical forest reserve have to be to ensure that most of its inhabitants will survive far into the future?

Clear-cuts, cow pastures, and croplands don't provide the food, shelter, or other requirements that forest creatures need to live. So when areas surrounding forest are cleared, the remaining forest becomes a wooded "island" in a sea of unsuitable habitat. Scientists studying islands in the ocean learned that large islands provide homes for more species than small islands. They also found that many wildlife populations on small islands eventually disappear. Might this pattern hold true for man-made islands of tropical forest?

In 1979, biologist Thomas Lovejoy started a giant experiment to find the answer. At that time, most landowners around Manaus, Brazil, were already clearing large areas in the Amazon rain forest to create pastures or farm fields. But the Brazilian government required that landowners retain a portion of their lands in natural forest. Lovejoy asked several ranchers to plan their clearings and natural forest

Clearing of tropical forests to create pasture and croplands makes the remaining forest patches into islands surrounded by a sea of pastures.

reserves in a way that would create forest patches of specific sizes. Over the next few years, the landowners created several square forest islands measuring 2.5, 25, and 254 acres. For comparison, a football field is about one acre in size.

Lovejoy coordinated a team of scientists to study the reserves and a nearby 25,400-acre parcel of undisturbed forest. The scientists examined the forest areas before any clearing was done, then recorded the changes that occurred after landowners removed the surrounding forests.

Changes began immediately. Sunlight suddenly streamed down to the floors of the forest islands, making them warmer and drier. The normally wet carpets of dead leaves began to crunch and crackle underfoot. Thunderstorm winds, once quelled by the unbroken expanse of trees, now rushed into the forest islands, breaking off branches and toppling weaker trees. These climate changes affected all parts of the smallest islands and extended two hundred to three hundred feet into the edges of the larger parcels—a distance equivalent to the length of two to three city buses. Many trees and other plants suffered as a result.

After about five years, tangled, dangling vines had formed a curtain around the edges of the forest islands. Their presence greatly diminished the climate

Thunderstorm winds broke off tree branches and toppled trees along the island edges. Sunlight suddenly streamed down onto the floor of the forest islands creating warmer, drier conditions.

changes. Nevertheless, over one-third of the plant life growing in the smaller forest islands died within ten years, and one-third of the plants growing along the edges of the larger plots died within seventeen years.

Lovejoy asked many kinds of scientists to help him compare the animal populations of intact forest with those in the forest islands. To accomplish this, mammalogists, herpetologists, ornithologists, and entomologists repeatedly visited the study sites before and after the forest-clearing. They surveyed the numbers and kinds of animals present using techniques appropriate for the animals they were studying. Investigating mammalogists determined the presence and abundance of mammals through direct observations and by searching for animal tracks and droppings. A herpetologist played recordings of frog vocalizations and recorded the kinds and numbers of frogs responding. Ornithologists set up nets of fine nylon mesh to capture small birds flitting about in the forest understory. These scientists compared the numbers and kinds of birds caught per hour in the forest plots.

Entomologists compared the numbers and kinds of butterflies observed per mile while walking along survey lines within each plot. To learn about dung beetle populations, they set out traps baited with animal droppings. They studied other ground beetle populations by setting out pitfall traps—small, open containers sunk into the forest floor. They set up stations baited with scented chemicals to compare the kinds and numbers of bees attracted. Though it was not possible to study all the kinds of animals present, the combined findings of these scientists painted a grim picture.

The mammalogists noted that signs of the largest mammals, including the margay cat, jaguar, mountain lion, paca, peccary, and deer quickly disappeared from all the forest islands. These animals must range through large areas of forest to find enough food, so their disappearance was not surprising.

Large mammals like jaguars disappeared from all the forest islands soon after the surrounding forests were cleared.

Groups of several kinds of monkeys remained in most forest islands at first. However, within two years after the surrounding areas were cleared, all monkeys disappeared from the 2.5-acre islands. All the large fruit-eating monkeys—the bearded sakis, capuchins, and black spider monkeys—disappeared from the 25 and 254-acre islands, too. Only a few groups of howler monkeys and small bands of golden-handed tamarins remained in any islands.

Black spider monkeys, bearded sakis, and capuchins disappeared from all the forest islands within two years after the surrounding forests were cleared.

Ten species of frogs occurred in the intact forest, but soon after clearing, only three species could be found in any of the forest islands. Three of the species that disappeared had used peccary wallows for breeding. The wallows disappeared because all the peccaries left soon after the surrounding forest was cleared. Without repeated digging by these animals, the shallow depressions soon filled in and dried out.

Ornithologists found that within a few years, about three-fourths of the insect-eating bird species of the intact forest had become less common in the 2.5- and 25-acre islands, and many species had disappeared entirely. One of the most striking changes was the disappearance of all the army ant–following bird species. These birds prey on insects scared out of hiding by army ant swarms.

Frog species that used peccary wallows for breeding disappeared from the forest islands when the peccary wallows dried up.

A single army ant colony requires about 76 acres of forest, so the 2.5- and 25-acre forest islands were too small to support even a single colony. The army ants soon died or moved out of these. Not surprisingly, all the army ant–following birds then disappeared, too. Both the army ants and ant-following birds were gone within two weeks after the surrounding forest was cleared.

The ornithologists expected that the 254-acre forest island would be able to support small numbers

Birds that follow army ants, including immaculate (1) and white-plumed (2) antbirds, disappeared from all the forest islands.

of ant-following birds, since it was large enough to support three army ant colonies. But the ant-following birds disappeared from even this large island soon after its isolation from the main forest. The scientists concluded that ant-following bird species must require more than three army ant colonies to help them find enough food.

Butterfly experts observed that ithomiine and satyrid butterfly species, which normally haunt the shadows of deep forest, gradually disappeared from the smaller forest islands. Sun-loving butterflies that usually live in forest clearings moved in.

Satyrid butterflies, which normally haunt the forest shadows, disappeared from the forest islands.

Beetle populations also changed. Several kinds of dung beetles became uncommon or disappeared from the forest islands. Investigating scientists think the change occurred because these insects feed on animal droppings. Since few large animals remained in the forest islands, there were fewer animal droppings for dung beetles to feed upon. Quite remarkably, the scientists found that animal droppings decayed more slowly in the forest islands than in undisturbed forest, due at least in part to the scarcity of dung beetles.

Insect scientists did not expect to find large reductions in other ground-dwelling beetle populations because individual beetles live within very small areas. But they were surprised. About one-half of the beetle species found in undisturbed forest disappeared from the 2.5-acre islands, and about one-third disappeared from the 25-acre islands. Even the large 254-acre forest

Several kinds of dung beetles and other ground-dwelling beetles soon became uncommon or disappeared entirely from the forest islands.

island lost about one-tenth of the ground-dwelling beetle species found in undisturbed forest. Curiously, the beetles that disappeared from the small islands were not rare kinds, but rather the species that were most common in undisturbed forest.

Biologists were particularly concerned to find that populations of many kinds of euglossine bees declined in the forest islands. These bees are important pollinators of a great variety of tropical forest plants, including many orchids, so they are sometimes called orchid bees. Large numbers of orchid bees responded to scented bait set out in undisturbed forest, but the smaller the forest island, the fewer bee species were attracted by the scents. Most of the orchid bees that turned up in the 2.5-acre forest islands were species that normally live in clearings.

Due to the great diversity of living creatures present, it was not possible to document all the changes in plant and animal populations that occurred in the forest

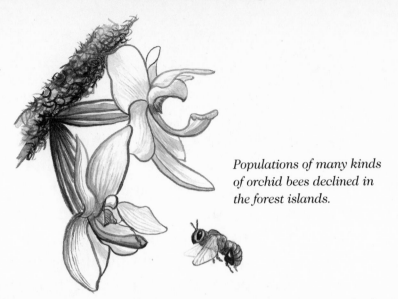

Populations of many kinds of orchid bees declined in the forest islands.

islands. But the changes scientists observed during this huge experiment clearly showed that many tropical forest animals—even tiny ones—require large forest areas.

The study also revealed how the loss of one species can ripple through an ecosystem, triggering a cascade of changes and species losses. The disappearance of peccaries led to the loss of frogs that had used peccary wallows for breeding. The loss of army ants led to the disappearance of ant-following birds. The disappearance of monkeys and other large mammals led to a decline in dung beetle numbers, which ultimately caused slower rates of decay.

Based on what is known about other interconnections in tropical forests, Lovejoy and other scientists predict that more species losses will occur over time in the forest islands. Botanists point out that many flowering plants in the forest islands are unlikely to form seeds if they require pollination by any of the missing orchid bees, or by ithomiine or satyrid butterflies that normally live in undisturbed forest. In addition, those fruiting plants that depend upon monkeys, other large fruit-eating animals, or dung beetles to spread their seeds will be unable to successfully reproduce in the forest islands. Consequently, many plant species are likely to slowly disappear from these fragments of the original forest. Because individual plants can live for twenty-five to two hundred years or more, individuals of some species will remain for a long time. But if they cannot form seeds, or if no seeds or young plants survive, these species will eventually be lost. The loss of any plant species will in turn affect all the forms of wildlife that depend upon it.

The results of Lovejoy's experiment clearly show that very large forest reserves are needed to ensure a future for a surprising variety of tropical forest creatures. More recent findings from this continuing experiment suggest that small forest islands could still be important for tropical forest wildlife protection over the long term.

Lovejoy and his colleagues originally hoped to track the changes in plant and animal populations within the forest islands for a hundred years or more. But they have had difficulty keeping the forest islands isolated. The ranchers who originally cleared the forest areas ran into trouble. Without the forest, the limited nutrients in the poor soil were soon used up and washed away. Without soil nutrients, most plants can't grow and cattle can find little to eat. So after a few years, several ranchers gave up on maintaining their pastures and croplands. Nature slowly began to reclaim their abandoned clearings.

By the late 1990s, some forest islands remained isolated. But new young trees were sprouting up around other plots. Among these were tree species that typically grow in the natural forest openings created whenever a large tree dies and falls over. Remarkably, some animal species have used these regrowing thickets of young trees as bridges back to the forest islands. This has modified the entirely depressing picture of rapidly disappearing species that first emerged from Lovejoy's study.

Most large mammals and many bird species are still missing from the forest islands. Beetle and butterfly populations remain distinctly altered. But due to the disappearance of predators, the number of small mammals such as opossums and mice in the small islands is now greater than the number found in undisturbed forest. Recent surveys show that a few species of forest frogs remain absent from the forest islands, but other kinds have survived. And the total number of frog species present has gone up because frog species that typically live in forest clearings and young forests have moved in. Hummingbird populations in some islands are now larger than those found in undisturbed forest. In addition, many ant-following bird species and other insect-eating bird species have returned to some of the "reconnected" islands. This indicates that army ants and possibly other previously missing insects have also returned. Orchid bee populations have apparently rebounded in some reconnected islands, too. Some of these long-term changes offer hope that the loss of species caused by forest fragmentation possibly could be reduced by maintaining corridors of regrowing forest to connect forest islands.

The regrowth of trees on the cleared lands also suggests that current forest losses need not all be permanent. Some forest losses could possibly be reversed. Often, as has happened near Manaus, tropical soils lose their productivity shortly after the forest is removed. As a result, people sometimes abandon their cleared lands. If large areas of undisturbed forest remain nearby, nature can sometimes partially reclaim these lands, allowing wildlife to return to previously isolated forest islands. If enough species return to forest islands and successfully reproduce, many of the broken connections among species could be rejoined. Eventually, instead of a continuing cascade of species losses, a renewed forest ecosystem might develop.

Some scientists think that if enough fragments and large expanses of tropical forest can be protected now, and eventually reconnected by corridors of regrowing forest, then healthy populations of many tropical forest wildlife could be maintained or restored. They think tropical forest restoration might even be possible in some regions where extensive clearing has already occurred. In the future, biologists and landowners may figure out ways to work together to plan clearings, regrowth areas, and reserves in rotating patterns that would balance limited human use of tropical forestlands with forest protection.

Due to the massive clearing occurring today, the tropical forests of the future will certainly be less extensive and less rich in animal and plant life than the forests that exist today. But reasons for hope exist. If we wisely use the knowledge gained through research, and if enough people care, we might yet save a good portion of the great diversity of life in tropical forests.

THE TROPICAL SYMPHONY

WITHOUT THE studies reported in this book as evidence, you might never suspect that tropical forest trees rely on birds, bats, monkeys, and even dung beetles to plant their seeds. You would not guess that wasps could protect bird nests or that some plants could trick insects. You wouldn't imagine that the survival of certain plants, butterflies, and even frogs might be intertwined with the survival of specific ants. Yet these curious connections are just a few of those that scientists have discovered in tropical forests of Central and South America alone. All around the world, research into the workings of these complex ecosystems has barely begun.

Once you perceive the many hidden connections, it is easy to understand that no single species can survive without many others. We cannot save jaguars, monkeys, toucans, orchids, or passionvines unless we also work to protect trees and epiphytes, small birds and bats, ants, wasps, dung beetles, and even fungi and microbes. The symphony of life that exists in tropical forests—and in nature all around us—depends upon the continued existence of a great orchestra of large and small creatures, and a myriad of interconnections.

LIST OF SELECTED REFERENCES

Scientists report their investigations and discoveries in professional journals available in most university libraries. This list of references includes some of the original reports of the scientists upon whose work this book is based.

Where Are All the Animals?
Elton, C. S. 1973. "The Structure of Invertebrate Populations Inside Neotropical Rain Forest." *Journal of Animal Ecology* 42: 55–104.

Emmons, L. H. 1984. "Geographic Variation in Densities and Diversities of Non-flying Mammals in Amazonia." *Biotropica* 16: 210–222.

Erwin, T. L. 1982. "Tropical Forests: Their Richness in Coleoptera and Other Arthropod Species." *Coleopterist's Bulletin* 36(1): 74–75.

Erwin, T. L., and Janice C. Scott. 1980. "Seasonal and Size Patterns, Trophic Structure, and Richness of Coleoptera in the Tropical Arboreal Ecosystem: The Fauna of the Tree *Luehea Seemannii* Triana and Planch in the Canal Zone of Panama." *Coleopterist's Bulletin* 34(3): 305–322.

Karr, J. R. 1971. "Structure of Avian Communities in Selected Panama and Illinois Habitats." *Ecological Monographs* 41(3): 207–229.

Owen, D. F. 1983. "The Abundance and Biomass of Forest Animals." In *Ecosystems of the World: Tropical Rainforest Ecosystems,* edited by F. B. Golley, pp 93–100. New York: Elsevier Scientific Publishing Co. 93–100.

Terborgh, J. 1986. "Keystone Plant Resources in the Tropical Forest." In *Conservation Biology,* edited by E. Soule, pp. 330–344. Sunderland, Mass.: Sinauer Associates.

Wilson, E. O. 1987. "The Arboreal Ant Fauna of Peruvian Amazon Forests: A First Assessment." *Biotropica* 19: 245–251.

The Case of the Monkeys That Fell From the Trees
Glander, K. E. 1975. "Habitat Description and Resource Utilization: A Preliminary Report on Mantled Howling Monkey Ecology." In *Socioecology and Psychology of Primates,* edited by R. H. Tuttle, pp. 37–57. The Hague: Mouton.

Glander, K. E. 1977. "Poison in a Monkey's Garden of Eden." *Natural History* 86(3): 35–41.

Glander, K. E. 1979. "Howling Monkey Feeding Behavior and Plant Secondary Compounds: A Study of Strategies." In *The Ecology of Arboreal Foliovores,* edited by G. G. Montgomery, pp. 561–574. Washington, D. C.: Smithsonian Institution Press.

Glander, K. E. 1982. "The Impact of Plant Secondary Compounds on Primate Feeding Behavior." *Yearbook of Physical Anthropology* 25: 1–18.

Glander, K. E. 1994. "Nonhuman Primate Self-medication with Wild Plant Foods." In *Eating on the Wild Side*, edited by N. L. Etkin, pp. 227–239. Tucson: University of Arizona Press.

The Mystery of the Ant-Plant's Army
Janzen, D. H. 1967. "Interaction of the Bull's Horn Acacia (*Acacia cornigera* L.) with an Ant Inhabitant *(Pseudomyrmex ferruginea* F. Smith) in Eastern Mexico." *University of Kansas Science Bulletin* 6: 315–558.

Janzen, D. H. 1966. "Coevolution of Mutualisms Between Ants and Acacias in Central America." *Evolution* 20: 249–275.

Tricksters in the Trees
Gilbert, L. E. 1971. "Butterfly-Plant Coevolution: Has *Passiflora adenopoda* Won the Selectional Race with Heliconiine butterflies?" *Science* 172: 585–586.

Gilbert, L. E. 1975. "Ecological Consequences of Coevolved Mutualism Between Butterflies and Plants." In *Coevolution of Animals and Plants,* edited by L. E. Gilbert and P. H. Raven, pp. 210–240. Austin: University of Texas Press.

Gilbert, L. E. 1982. "The Coevolution of a Butterfly and a Vine." *Scientific American* 247(2): 110–121.

Gilbert, L. E. 1983. "Coevolution and Mimicry." In *Coevolution,* edited by D. J. Futuyma and M. Slatkin, pp. 264–281. Sunderland, Mass.: Sinauer Associates.

Williams, K. S., and L. E. Gilbert. l981. "Insects as Selective Agents on Plant Vegetative Morphology: Egg Mimicry Reduces Egg-laying by Butterflies." *Science* 212: 467–469.

The Search for a Deadly Frog's Poisons

Daly, J. W. 1995. "The Chemistry of Poisons in Amphibian Skin." *Proceedings of the National Academy of Sciences U.S.A.* 92: 9–13.

Daly, J. W., H. M. Garraffo, and C. W. Myers. 1997. "The Origin of Frog Skin Alkaloids: An Enigma." *Pharmaceutical News* 4: 9–14.

Daly, J. W., H. M. Garraffo, T. F. Spande, C. Jaramillo, and A. S. Rand. 1994. "Dietary Source for Skin Alkaloids of Poison Frogs (Dendrobatidae)?" *Journal of Chemical Ecology* 20: 943–955.

Daly, J. W., H. M. Garraffo, P. Jain, T. F. Spande, R. R. Snelling, C. Jaramillo, and A. S. Rand. 2000. "Arthropod-Frog Connection: Decahydroquinoline and Pyrrolizidine Alkaloids Common to Microsympatric Myrmicine Ants and Dendrobatid Frogs." *Journal of Chemical Ecology* 26(1): 73–85.

Daly, J. W., S. I. Secunda, H. M. Garraffo, T. F. Spande, A. Wisnieski, C. Nishihira, and J. F. Cover, Jr. 1992. "Variability in Alkaloid Profiles in Neotropical Poison Frogs (Dendrobatidae): Genetic Versus Environmental Determinants." *Toxicon* 30(8): 887–898.

Daly, J. W., S. I. Secunda, H. M. Garraffo, T. F. Spande, A. Wisnieski, and J. F. Cover, Jr. 1994. "An Uptake System for Dietary Alkaloids in Poison Frogs (Dendrobatidae). *Toxicon* 32: 637–663.

The Curious Case of the Helpful Parasites

Smith, N. G. 1968. "The Advantage of Being Parasitized." *Nature* 219: 690–694.

163

Smith, N. G. 1979. "Alternate Responses by Hosts to Parasites Which May Be Helpful or Harmful." In *Encounter: The Interface Between Populations,* edited by B. Nikol., pp. 7–15. New York: Academic Press.

Smith, N. G. 1980. "Some Evolutionary, Ecological, and Behavioral Correlates of Communal Nesting by Birds with Wasps or Bees." In *Acta. XVII Congressus Internationalis Ornithologica.* Berlin: Verlag der Deutschen Ornithologen Gesellschaft, 1199–1205.

The Butterflies' Strange Pursuit
Ray, T. S., and C. C. Andrews. 1980. "Ant Butterflies: Butterflies That Follow Army Ants to Feed on Antbird Droppings." *Science* 210: 1147–4.

The Case of the Winged Fruit Thieves
Howe, H. F. 1977. "Bird Activity and Seed Dispersal of a Tropical Wet Forest Tree." *Ecology* 58: 539–550.

Howe, H. F., and J. Smallwood. 1982. "Ecology of Seed Dispersal." *Annual Review of Ecology and Systematics* 13: 201–228.

Janzen, D. H. 1971. "Seed Predation by Animals." *Annual Review of Ecology and Systematics* 2: 465–492.

The Mystery in the Monkey Dung
Estrada, A., and R. Coates-Estrada. 1984. "Fruit-eating and Seed Dispersal by Howling Monkeys (*Alouatta palliata*) in the Tropical Rain Forest of Los Tuxtlas, Mexico." *American Journal of Primatology* 6: 77–91.

Estrada, A., and R. Coates-Estrada. 1986. "Frugivory by Howling Monkeys at Los Tuxtlas, Mexico: Dispersal and Fate of Seeds." In *Frugivores and Seed Dispersal,* edited by A. Estrada and T. H. Fleming, pp. 93–104. Dordrecht: Dr. W. Junk Publishers.

Estrada, A., and R. Coates-Estrada. 1991. "Howling Monkeys (*Alouatta palliata*), Dung Beetles (Scarabaeidae) and Seed Dispersal: Ecological Interactions in the Tropical Rain Forest of Los Tuxtlas, Mexico." *Journal of Tropical Ecology* 7: 459–474.

The Mystery of the Unknown Pollinators

Kearns, C. A., and D. W. Inouye. 1997. "Pollinators, Flowering Plants, and Conservation Biology." *Bioscience* 47 (5): 297–307.

Machado, I. C., and A. V. Lopes. 2000. "*Souroubea guianensis* Aubl.: Quest for Its Legitimate Pollinator and the First Record of Tapetal Oil in the Marcgraviaceae." *Annals of Botany* 85: 705–711.

How Much Forest Is Enough?
Becker, P., Moure, J. S., and F. J. A. Peralta. 1991. "More About Euglossine Bees in Amazonian Forest Fragments." *Biotropica* 23: 586–591.

Didham, R. K., P. M. Hammond, J. H. Lawton, P. Eggleton, and N. E. Stork. 1998. "Beetle Species Responses to Tropical Forest Fragmentation." *Ecological Monographs* 68(3): 295–323.

Ferreira, L. V., and W. F. Laurance. 1997. "Effects of Forest Fragmentation on Mortality and Damage of Selected Trees in Central Amazonia." *Conservation Biology* 11(3): 797–801.

Hagan, J. M., W. M. Vander Haegen, and P. S. McKinley. 1996. "The Early Development of Forest Fragmentation Effects on Birds." *Conservation Biology* 10(1): 188–202.

Klein, B. C. 1989. "Effects of Forest Fragmentation on Dung and Carrion Beetle Communities in Central Amazonia." *Ecology* 70(6): 1715–1725.

Laurance, W. F., and R. O. Bierregaard, Jr., editors. 1997. *Tropical Forest Remnants: Ecology, Management and Conservation of Fragmented Communities.* Chicago: University of Chicago Press.

Laurance, W. F., L. V. Ferreira, J. M. Rankin-de Merona, and Susan G. Laurance. 1998. "Rainforest Fragmentation and the Dynamics of Amazonian Tree Communities." *Ecology* 79(6): 2032–2040.

Laurance, W. F., S. G. Laurance, L. V. Ferreira, J. M. Rankin-de Merona, C. Gascon, T. E. Lovejoy. 1997. "Biomass Collapse in Amazonian Forest Fragments." *Science* 278: 1117–1118.

Lovejoy, T. E., et. al. R. O. Bierregaard, Jr., A. B. Rylands, J. R. Malcolm,

C. E. Quintela, L. H. Harper, K. S. Brown, Jr., A. H. Powell, G. V. N. Powell, H. O. R. Schubart, and M. B. Hayes. 1986. "Edge and Other Effects of Isolation on Amazon Forest Fragments." In *Conservation Biology: The Science of Scarcity and Diversity,* edited by M. Soule, pp. 257–285. Sunderland, Mass.: Sinauer Associates.

Lovejoy, T. E., J. M. Rankin, R. O. Bierregaard, Jr., K. S. Brown, Jr., L. H. Emmons, and M. E. Van der Voort. 1984. "Ecosystem Decay of Amazon Forest Remnants." In *Extinction,* edited by M. H. Nitecki, pp. 294–325. Chicago: University of Chicago Press.

Stouffer, P. C., and R. O. Bierregaard, Jr. 1995. "Use of Amazonian Forest Fragments by Understory Insectivorous Birds." *Ecology* 76(8): 2429–2445.

INDEX